Tilly Bagshawe is the internationally bestselling author of eight previous novels. A teenage single mother at 17, Tilly won a place at Cambridge University and took her baby daughter with her. She went on to enjoy a successful career in The City before becoming a writer. As a journalist, Tilly contributed regularly to the *Sunday Times*, *Daily Mail* and *Evening Standard* before following in the footsteps of her sister Louise and turning her hand to novels.

Tilly's first book, *Adored*, was a smash hit on both sides of the Atlantic and she hasn't looked back since. Tilly and her family divide their time between their homes in Los Angeles and their beach house on Nantucket Island.

Tilly Bagshawe

ONE CHRISTMAS MORNING

HARPER

Harper
An imprint of HarperCollins*Publishers*
77-85 Fulham Palace Road
London, W6 8JB

www.harpercollins.co.uk

This paperback edition 2014
1

First published in Great Britain by
HarperCollins*Publishers* 2013

Copyright © Tilly Bagshawe 2013

Tilly Bagshawe asserts the moral right to
be identified as the author of this work

A catalogue record for this book is
available from the British Library

ISBN: 978-0-00-812117-4

Set in Meridien by Palimpsest Book Production Limited,
Falkirk, Stirlingshire

CHAPTER ONE

'All right, Michael, let's try it again, shall we? And this time maybe *without* the finger up your nose.'

Laura Tiverton gave what she hoped was an encouraging smile to the six-year-old boy on stage. The child glared back at her sullenly. For a Christmas angel in the Fittlescombe village Nativity play, Michael O'Brien was sadly lacking in festive spirit. Not that Laura blamed him for that. At this point she wanted nothing more than to go home, lock the door, pour herself an enormous Laphroaig and eat an entire bowl of Cadbury's chocolate buttons in front of *Downton Abbey*.

'"We Three Kings of Orient Are", from the top.' She forced the jollity into her voice as Mrs Bramdean launched into the familiar chords on St Hilda's Primary School's famously out-of-tune piano. *What on earth possessed me to agree to direct this fiasco?* Laura thought despairingly. *I'm a screenwriter, not a schoolteacher. I don't even* like *children.* Then she thought about the baby she'd miscarried in the summer – John's baby – and for the hundredth time that week found herself fighting back tears.

1

Twenty-eight years old, with a mane of curly hair the same blue-black as a crow's feathers, pale skin and soulful, dark eyes like two wells of oil, Laura Tiverton was both attractive and successful. After three years spent working as a writer on two BBC dramas, last year she'd finally produced a pilot of her own, a show about a newly qualified teacher from the shires left to sink or swim in a failing inner-city comprehensive school. Although the series wasn't ultimately commissioned, Laura was already winning praise for herself as an innovative and talented young TV writer. Her love affair with the BBC's very handsome, very married Head of Drama, John Bingham, had only served to raise her profile further as one of the corporation's brilliantly rising stars.

And then last spring, in one fell swoop, it had all gone horribly wrong. Laura fell unexpectedly pregnant. Although the baby wasn't planned, she'd been delighted, believing John Bingham's assurances that he loved her, that his marriage had been over for years, and that he only stayed with Felicia because of their children, now all in their late teens.

'You've done the right thing for so long, darling,' Laura told him over dinner, the night she did the test. 'But now we'll have a child of our own to think of. Don't you think it's time you made the split with Felicia official?'

John looked so noble and concerned across the table, his chiselled features somehow even handsomer at fifty than they had been in his youth. There was a wisdom about him, a maturity and solidity that Laura found sexy and reassuring at the same time. He mumbled something about timings and 'being sensitive to everyone involved', and Laura thought, *He'll make a wonderful father. I'm so lucky*.

The next morning Laura was fired. Her show was cancelled, the producer citing 'creative issues'. When Laura tried to call John to remonstrate, she discovered he'd changed his mobile number. His embarrassed PA, Caroline, refused even to give Laura an appointment to see him.

'I'm so sorry. His schedule's er . . . well it's terribly full. Maybe in a month or two. When things have settled down.'

Reeling with shock, Laura had committed the cardinal sin of calling her lover at home. She would never forget the strained, tearful voice on the other end of the line.

'If you're that girl, the one trying to blackmail my husband, you can jolly well go away! You won't get a penny out of him. And you won't destroy this family either.'

John had always described his wife as distant and 'completely uninterested' in their marriage. This poor woman sounded utterly distraught. Hanging up, shaking, Laura could still hear John's voice, mellow and reassuring: 'Truly, Laura, my darling, it's a business arrangement, nothing more. Felicia knows we're both free agents. It's you I love.'

Heartbroken and embarrassed, Laura determined to keep the baby anyway. But a miscarriage at eleven weeks put an end to those dreams too.

'You're young,' the doctor said kindly. 'You can try again.'

Laura went home and cried for a week. Then, unable to stand one more hour in the Battersea flat that had been her and John's love-nest, she'd picked up the phone, found a six-month rental in Fittlescombe, the idyllic South Downs village where her granny used to live and where Laura had spent so many happy summers as a child, and left. Left London, left John, left her entire mess of a life.

I'll write a masterpiece. I'll recuperate. I'll learn to cook and buy a dog and give up alcohol and go for long runs in the fresh air.

She managed the dog part, and now shared her home and so-called life with a fat, chronically lazy but endearing pug named Peggy. And she had done a bit of writing, in between fixing Briar Cottage's leaky roof, dodgy electrics and jerry-rigged plumbing, as installed in 1932 and not 'fiddled with' since. But her latest play was certainly no masterpiece. Truth be told, after five months it was still little more than notes and a few character sketches. As for the healthy country lifestyle, Laura's only runs so far had been to and from the larder, with Peggy waddling eagerly in her wake. If God had intended Laura Tiverton to bake, he would not have invented Mr Kipling. And, if he'd intended her to be sober, he wouldn't have broken her heart.

'Miss Tiverton. Miss *Tiverton*!'

Michael O'Brien's howls brought Laura back to the present with an unpleasant bump.

'I need the toilet.'

'All right, Michael, off you go.'

'I need to do a poo.'

'All right, Michael. Thank you.'

'Right now! It's starting to come out . . .'

'Oh, Jesus.'

Thankfully, Eileen Carter, Michael's class teacher, rushed onto the stage and whisked the star soloist off to the loo before disaster struck.

Harry Hotham, St Hilda's headmaster for the last fifteen years and the biggest flirt in Fittlescombe, saw his chance, sidling up to Laura and slipping a lecherous arm around her waist.

'You know what they say, my dear. Never work with animals or children. I'm afraid with a village Nativity play, you're rather saddled with both, ha ha!'

It was less of a laugh, more of a bray. Despite being drenched in Penhaligon's aftershave, Harry Hotham still managed to smell of sweat and arousal, the familiar scent of the older Lothario at work. It reminded Laura of John so acutely, she gagged.

'Yes, well, the children's rehearsals are over now for the day,' she said, wriggling free from the headmaster's vicelike grip. 'Mary, Joseph and the shepherds should be here at any moment for a read-through.'

'Indeed, indeed. Well, I won't keep you,' said Harry Hotham, staring unashamedly at Laura's breasts beneath her tight-fitting cashmere sweater. 'I must buy you dinner some time though, my dear, to thank you properly for stepping in as our director.'

'There's really no need, Harry.'

'No need? Nonsense. There's every need. We're expecting great things this year, you know, Laura. Great things.'

I *was expecting great things*, thought Laura, as St Hilda's headmaster shuffled out with the remaining children and teachers. *A baby. Marriage. But here I am in a draughty old church hall, trying to wrangle defecating six-year-olds while men old enough to be my father invite my tits to dinner.*

'Oh. You're here.'

Laura spun around, her heart already sinking. Gabriel Baxter, a.k.a. Joseph, a.k.-also-a. the bane of Laura Tiverton's existence since rehearsals began two weeks ago, looked at her as if she were something unpleasant he'd forgotten to wipe off his shoe.

'Of course I'm here. I'm the director. Where else would I be?'

Gabe shrugged and grabbed himself a chair. 'A man can hope.'

Laura remembered Gabe from summers spent in Fittlescombe as a little girl. He was an arrogant, irritating little shit back then, and he clearly hadn't changed, improbably claiming not to remember Laura at all, despite their frequent childhood run-ins.

'I can't be expected to remember every tourist who ever came to the village,' he remarked dismissively at the Parish Council meeting, when Harry Hotham introduced Laura as this year's Nativity play director.

Like many Fittlescombe locals, Gabe Baxter resented the fact that his village had become a Mecca for second-homers and wealthy London media types. Two of the prettiest local manor houses had been bought by famous actresses, and a third belonged to a Russian industrialist whose supermodel wife had attracted unwanted paparazzi to Fittlescombe's peaceful high street.

'I wasn't a *tourist*,' Laura retorted crossly. 'I came here every summer. Granny lived at Mill House for over twenty years.'

'Oh! "Granny lived at Mill House", did she? Over twenty ye-ahs?' Gabe mocked Laura's upper-class accent perfectly, and she remembered instantly why she'd always loathed him. 'Well, one must excuse the likes of us poor servants for not remembering everything about Granny's domestic arrangements.'

What grated most was that Gabriel Baxter was hardly a 'poor servant', for all his class-war rhetoric. A working farmer, Gabe owned a valuable property on the outskirts of the village and drove a Land Rover Defender. Whereas Laura rented a cottage on the brink of being condemned, was officially unemployed and drove a Fiat Punto so old and knackered that the passenger door had been welded shut.

'Please don't tell me it's just us. I've had a long enough day as it is.' Reaching up, Gabe rubbed his neck wearily. Even in November, he still sported a farmer's tan, his face bronzed as much from windburn as from the sun. Blond

6

and broad, with a stocky frame and the powerful shoulders of a shire horse, there was something mischievous about him that people generally, and women especially, found irresistible. That irked Laura too. The fact that Gabe was so popular in the village, so eminently capable of warmth and humour and kindness – just not towards her. Well, he could stick his reverse snobbery up his arse, along with the giant chip on his shoulder. She wasn't about to let him rile her. Not today.

'Thankfully, Lisa and the others will be here in a moment,' she said, smiling through gritted teeth. 'Perhaps, if my instructions are a bit too tricky for you to follow, they'll be able to translate. I'll ask one of the shepherds to draw you a picture.'

Gabe was about to say something when Lisa James, this year's Mary, walked in. Wearing a cut-off Metallica T-shirt and skintight jeans that enveloped her perfectly round bottom like clingfilm round a pair of peaches, the barmaid from Fittlescombe's famous Fox Inn looked anything but virginal. Turning away from Laura, Gabe flashed his co-star a hundred-megawatt smile.

'Hello, darling.' He winked. 'Come and sit with your husband while Her Royal Highness over there gets organized. She'll be putting us through our paces in a minute, won't you, Miss Tiverton?'

Laura sighed. She felt deeply tired all of a sudden. She'd had enough of petulant children for one day.

By the time her mechanically challenged Fiat Punto spluttered to a halt outside Briar Cottage, darkness had long since fallen. It was November, and the nights were already bitterly cold. Behind Laura, the winding lanes of the village were slick with rain that by morning would have turned to sheet ice. In front of her, behind Briar Cottage, the South Downs rose like dark, shadowy giants. In the daytime the chalk hills looked benevolent, a bed of lush green pillows protecting the house from harm, cushioning Laura from the slings and arrows of modern life. She felt wonderfully safe here, enveloped not just by the peaceful rural setting of Fittlescombe, but by her own childhood, by happier times. This village, set deep in the Swell Valley, had always been her sanctuary, a magical, intoxicating place.

But now, in the darkness, and with Gabriel Baxter's snide remarks still ringing in her ears, the Downs seemed to jump out at her, looming threateningly like an uncertain future. Holding the Nativity play script over her head as a makeshift umbrella, Laura dashed up the garden path and ran inside, slamming the front door closed behind her.

Peggy the pug heaved her fat form out of the basket by the Aga and waddled over to greet her mistress, wiggling her stump of a tail.

'Hello, Peg.' Pulling a McVitie's chocolate digestive out of the jar on the counter, Laura ate half and gave half to the dog. 'At least *you're* pleased to see me.'

It was the kitchen at Briar Cottage that had sold Laura on the place. That and the overgrown garden that had looked riotously beautiful in spring, with dog roses everywhere and hollyhocks reaching almost to the chimneys, but now, in winter, untended by Laura, was a sodden mess of brambles and weeds. The kitchen maintained its charm, however, with its uneven flagstones worn smooth from centuries of use, its cheery red Aga and the cushioned window seat looking out over the rooftops of Fittlescombe with St Hilda's Church steeple just visible in the distance. It was impossible not to feel cheered walking into Briar Cottage's kitchen, even with the November rain peeing down outside, and your script hopelessly unfinished, and the village Nativity play you had stupidly, *stupidly* agreed to direct shaping up to be the biggest fiasco in Fittlescombe since the Black Death.

Propped up next to the biscuit jar was the stiff, embossed invitation that had arrived this morning. Picking it up, Laura read it again, as surprised now as she had been when she'd first opened it:

Rory Flint-Hamilton, Esq., requests the pleasure of the
company of
Miss Laura Tiverton
At Furlings Christmas Hunt Ball
Friday 23 December, 8 p.m.
Black Tie
RSVP Furlings, Fittlescombe

Rory Flint-Hamilton was what an earlier generation would have described as the lord of the manor. Owners of the magnificent Furlings Estate, unquestionably the most beautiful house in the entire Swell Valley, Rory Flint-Hamilton's ancestors had once owned the entire village of Fittlescombe. Nine generations of Flint-Hamiltons lay buried in St Hilda's churchyard. Unlike those of most grand old country families, the Flint-Hamiltons' fortunes and influence had risen, rather than fallen, in modern times, thanks to canny investments by Rory's father Hugo in a number of African mines. Now an old man himself, and never a go-getter like his father, Rory Flint-Hamilton was content with the quiet life of a country squire. Every year, however, he bridged the divide between Fittlescombe's old guard and its newer, more glamorous part-time residents by hosting the Furlings Hunt Ball, an event so grand that prime ministers and even the occasional Hollywood film star had been known to attend.

How on earth Laura had scored an invitation she had no idea. Her grandmother had known the Flint-Hamiltons, of course, but the two families had never been close. Laura herself had only ever seen Rory Flint-Hamilton at church, and was pretty certain she had never spoken to him. Perhaps Harry Hotham had said something. Or the vicar, dear old Reverend Slaughter. This morning, excited to receive the card, Laura had impetuously posted the news of her invitation on Facebook. But, as the day wore on, the horrible thought occurred to her that perhaps local people felt sorry for her. She could picture St Hilda's headmaster now, cornering Rory Flint-Hamilton in the village stores:

'Pretty girl, but terribly lonely. *Do* ask her, old man. She needs to get out.'

Putting down the card with a shudder, Laura tried to think about supper. Deciding she was too tired to cook or even set a place for herself, she kicked off her shoes, grabbed four more chocolate biscuits out of the jar and trudged upstairs to run a bath. In London she'd always kept her flat scrupulously clean, just in case John decided to pop in unannounced. Here she thought nothing of dropping her clothes in a heap on the bathroom floor and leaving a trail of biscuit crumbs on the stairs. No one was going to see the mess, any more than anyone was going to see her unshaven legs and woefully unpedicured toes, or the small but definitely there roll of fat that had formed around her middle like a flotation device. *Saving me from drowning in heartbreak*, thought Laura. Then she thought how much fatter she'd be if she were still pregnant – she'd be almost ready to pop by now – and had to splash water on her face to stop herself from crying.

Five minutes later the bath was ready. Sinking her aching limbs into the hot, lavender-scented bathwater, Laura exhaled deeply, relaxed for the first time all day. Dangling her hand over the side of the bath, so Peggy could lick the chocolate from her fingers, she thought idly about Gabriel Baxter and Lisa James – Joseph and Mary. They were probably back at Gabe's farm, having wild sex right this minute. For a split second Laura felt a pang of envy. Not because she had the slightest desire to sleep with Gabe, but because, since John and losing the baby, she hadn't the slightest desire, full stop. She was only twenty-eight. But there were days when she couldn't imagine ever being sexual again.

'I'm turning into an old woman, Peggy.'

The pug snuffled dismissively. Or perhaps it was supportively. Peggy did a lot of snuffling. Lying back, Laura immersed her whole head in the water, allowing her dark curls to spread out around her like a mermaid's locks, luxuriating in the warmth and peace. When she sat up again, the phone was ringing.

'Goddamn it.' She contemplated not answering. It was probably just that old pervert Harry Hotham, trying to pin her down for a dinner date. Disgusting old goat. But years spent in the cut and thrust of a TV studio had left her congenitally incapable of leaving telephones to ring. Pulling herself up out of the bath like a Kraken, dripping lavender water all over the oak floorboards, she skidded down the corridor into her bedroom. Just as she was about to pick up the phone, the answer machine kicked in. She heard her own voice played back to her.

'This is Laura. Please leave a message.'

God, I sound awful. So depressed! I must remember to do a perkier version in the morning.

'Laura, hi. This is Daniel.'

She froze. *Daniel. Daniel Smart?* Daniel Smart was an old flame – a very old flame – from her student days at Oxford. Head of the Boat Club, and president of OUDS, the

11

prestigious university dramatic society, Daniel had always been destined to do great things. They'd had a fling in the Christmas of Laura's second year – they'd actually spent the holiday at Fittlescombe, in the cottage at Mill House, the year before Laura's parents sold it. When the romance fizzled out, Laura had been briefly heartbroken. But it all felt like a lifetime ago now. Last she heard, Daniel was a wildly successful West End theatre producer. Married. Happy.

'Look, one of our old Oxford lot told me you were in Fittlescombe.' He laughed nervously. 'I know I shouldn't. But I came over all nostalgic. Anyway, probably silly of me. I just thought I'd get back in touch, see how you are.'

Laura sank down on the bed, shivering. In her haste, she'd forgotten a towel. The Aga kept the kitchen warm, but what little central heating there was upstairs at Briar Cottage all seeped out through the warped and rotting windows. Laura's bedroom was as cold as any polar base camp. Pulling the knitted bedspread off the bed, she wrapped it around herself.

'Well.' Daniel laughed again. 'If you *do* want to call, I'm on 07891 991 686. But if not, and you think I'm a complete lunatic, I quite understand. I probably am. Love anyway. Er . . . bye.'

There was a click. Laura stared at the red flashing light in the answer machine for a long time, too stunned to move.

Daniel. Daniel Smart had called her! Tracked her down, here of all places. As if that weren't bizarre enough, he'd sounded so *awkward*. Almost shy. The Daniel Laura remembered was supremely confident. Never in a million years would he have left her a message like that back in the old days. She, Laura, had been the nervous one, the one who couldn't believe her luck that the likes of Daniel Smart might be interested in *her*.

Maybe he'd changed. Maybe time had softened him.

Perhaps Daniel Smart had also been through some tough times. *Like me.*

Laura pulled the bedspread more tightly around her and, quite spontaneously, smiled.

Perhaps, at long, long last, her luck was about to change.

CHAPTER TWO

'No, no, no and no. I am not spending four thousand pounds on a lump of ice.'

Rory Flint-Hamilton pushed aside his boiled egg bad-temperedly. It was too early for this nonsense.

'With respect, Mr Flint-Hamilton, it's hardly a "lump". This would be a life-size, intricately carved statue of Eros. It would make a spectacular centrepiece for the hunt ball.'

'I daresay. But the next morning it'll be a four-thousand-pound puddle. I'm not the Aga Khan, you know, Mrs Worsley. We'll have a nice vase of flowers like we usually do. Ask Jennings for some roses and whatnot.'

The Furlings housekeeper knew when she was beaten. It was the same every year. Mr Flint-Hamilton wanted to do everything on a shoestring, grumbling and moaning about the expense of the ball like Fittlescombe's own Mr Scrooge. But somehow, thanks in no small part to Mrs Worsley's ingenuity, they always pulled off an event to be proud of.

While the housekeeper cleared away his breakfast, Rory Flint-Hamilton gazed out of the window across Furlings

Park. It was a vile day, grey and drizzly, with a vicious wind whipping at the bare oak trees and flattening the sodden grass. But Furlings's grounds still looked magical, a carpet of vivid green spotted with deer that had lived on the estate for as long as the Flint-Hamilton family themselves.

Rory was in his early seventies but looked older. Tall and wiry, he walked with a stoop and sported a shock of hair so white it almost looked like a wig. His eyebrows were also white and grown out to an inordinate length, something Rory was secretly proud of, curling them with his fingers the way a Victorian magician might have twirled his moustache. Since his much younger wife, Vicky, had died five years ago in a car accident, Rory had aged overnight, embracing old age like a young man rushing into the arms of a lover. Rory and Vicky's only child, their daughter Tatiana, was living in London now and rarely came home. There was no one to stay young for, no one who cared whether or not Rory went to bed at nine every night and spent entire afternoons eating fudge and watching the racing on television. He was increasingly reclusive, and so the Furlings Hunt Ball was the one time of year when Rory Flint-Hamilton was forced to engage with the outside world. He always dreaded it. This year, thanks to Tati's behaviour, he was dreading it more than most.

Once Mrs Worsley had left the room, he reopened the offending page of the *Daily Mail*. Once again, his daughter was in the gossip pages. This time she was accused of stealing the husband of a minor member of the Royal Family and cavorting with him at a nightclub in Mayfair. The pictures of them together turned Rory's stomach. The man was old enough to be Tati's father and looked a fool in jeans and a silk shirt unbuttoned to the chest. As for Tati's skirt, Rory

15

had seen bigger handkerchiefs. It was clear from the photo-graph that Tati was very, very drunk.

She's twenty-three, for God's sake; she's not a teenager any more. When is she going to grow up?

Rory Flint-Hamilton was not a demonstrative man. But he loved his daughter deeply, and hated watching her throw away her potential and talents on an empty life of partying as she dragged the Flint-Hamilton name through the mud. He also took his role as custodian of Furlings very seriously. He wasn't going to live for ever. The thought of handing the estate down to Tatiana filled Rory with a fear so acute, it was hard to breathe.

Folding up the newspaper and putting it under his arm, he got up and shuffled slowly out into the hall. A long, marble-floored corridor lined with Flint-Hamilton family portraits led to what had always been known as the 'Great Room', a vast, galleried ballroom with eight-foot sash windows affording a spectacular view of the Downs. In only six weeks' time, this room would be filled with noise and laughter, bedecked with dark-green holly, blood-red berries and plump, white mistletoe. A towering Christmas tree, cut from the estate's own woodland, would sparkle beneath the light of the chandelier. Furlings would come back to life, for one night only, the huntsmen in their cheery red coats, and the rest of the men in black tie, with the women dressed to the nines in ball gowns and jewels, clattering across the marble in their high-heeled shoes like a troupe of tap dancers.

Vicky would have outshone all of them.

As for Tatiana, who looked so like her mother it was painful . . . Rory Flint-Hamilton closed his eyes and said a silent prayer. *Please let Tati behave herself. I couldn't face another scandal. Not here.*

He would send her an email today, telling her in no uncertain terms that her married duke was absolutely not welcome. The rest of the world may have gone to hell in a handbasket. But the Furlings Hunt Ball would remain a bastion of tradition and propriety. Rory Flint-Hamilton intended to make sure of it.

Daniel Smart gazed out of the train window, sipping his disappointingly watery hot chocolate and glad he was in the warmth of a first-class carriage and not outside in the cold and wet.

The last time he'd been to Fittlescombe, he'd been in his final year at Oxford. It was at Christmastime, and he remembered how struck he'd been by the beauty of the village, blanketed in snow, the flint cottages nestled tightly together beneath a crisp, bright-blue winter sky. He and Laura Tiverton had been lovers then. They'd spent a joyous holiday together in the gardener's cottage at Mill House, making love by the fire and drinking mulled wine and going for long, romantic walks in the snow.

Christ, that was a long time ago.

So much had happened since that Christmas. Daniel's career had taken off spectacularly. He now had two West End plays under his belt and a third in production. He'd got married to Rachel, had two little boys, Milo and Alexis. And now, at thirty, he was getting divorced, painfully and expensively. As the train clattered on through the Sussex countryside, he wondered whether Laura's life had been similarly eventful in the eight years since he'd seen her last. He'd been nervous, leaving her a voicemail, afraid he'd come across like a stalker or a weirdo. But, when she'd returned his call the next day, she'd sounded so happy to hear from him, so warm and welcoming, that all his fears evaporated.

She'd immediately suggested meeting, and didn't flinch when Daniel proposed that, rather than her coming to London, he would jump on a train to Fittlescombe 'for old times' sake'. Her voice hadn't changed at all, and instantly took him back to those happy, student days. Rather ungallantly, he found himself hoping that the same could be said for her figure. Most of the girls he knew at Oxford had turned into serious heifers since college. Then again, they'd all had babies. Laura Tiverton was still unmarried and gloriously child-free.

At last the train pulled up at Fittlescombe station. There was no snow this time, only grey drizzle and a wind that sliced at Daniel's face like a razor blade as he stepped onto the platform. A lone figure in a thick Puffa jacket, woolly hat and multiple scarves stood next to the ticket office. They were so swaddled in layers of clothing, they could have been male or female, fat or thin, old or young.

'Laura?'

'Daniel!'

They hugged awkwardly. Laura looked at his thin sports jacket, worn over a tight-fitting cashmere sweater in duck-egg blue. 'Aren't you cold?'

'Bloody freezing.' He grinned. 'Where's your car?'

He was every bit as handsome as Laura remembered him, tall and fit with thick chestnut hair and eyes the same dark green as the baize on the snooker table in the Balliol College bar.

'Follow me. It's a bit of a banger, I'm afraid. I'm between jobs at the moment so I'm, er, economizing.'

Daniel squeezed himself into the tiny Fiat Punto. His legs were so long they practically touched the ceiling. 'Please tell me you live close by.'

He looked ridiculous, doubled over in the passenger seat.

Laura burst out laughing. 'Five minutes, honestly. I'll drive fast.'

As they hurtled along the back lanes of Fittlescombe, Daniel's attention was divided between looking at Laura – he couldn't assess her figure beneath the enormous coat, but her skin still looked flawless and the dark curls and almost-black eyes were just as he remembered them – and the village itself, picture-perfect despite the awful weather. No wonder so many influential people from the theatre and TV worlds chose to live out here. It was only an hour and a half from London by train, but it was a different world.

It was four o'clock and darkness was already starting to set in by the time they pulled up in front of Briar Cottage. But if anything the twilight enhanced its decrepit charms. Lights blazed cosily from the downstairs windows, and a thin trail of smoke from Laura's afternoon fire snaked up into the air above the sloping roof.

'Wow. Pretty. It looks like every writer's dream. You must be so productive out here.'

'Oh, definitely,' Laura lied. It wouldn't do to sound like a failure in front of Daniel. He didn't need to know that she'd spent half of this morning watching *Deal or No Deal* on television and the other half stuffing dirty laundry into drawers and cupboards so Daniel didn't think she'd become a total slattern. Not that she expected anything to happen between them. Or even *wanted* anything to happen. It was too soon after John.

Inside, Daniel dropped his overnight bag on the floor and took off his jacket, watching out of the corner of his eye as Laura peeled off layer after layer of clothing. Unwrapped to a pair of black corduroy trousers and a chocolate-brown sweater, she was plumper than she had been at Oxford, but definitely still foxy. Thankfully, at least half of the extra weight seemed to have gone on her boobs.

'Let me take that.' She reached for his jacket, opening the hall cupboard, then closing it again quickly when an assorted medley of dirty wellies, scrunched-up coats and dog chews tumbled out of it onto the floor. 'It's a lovely cottage but there's not as much storage as I'd like.' Laura blushed.

She's still sexy, thought Daniel.

'We'll hang it in your room. Come on up.'

Following her up the narrow cottage staircase, admiring the curve of her bottom in the slightly too-tight cords, Daniel found himself being led into a low-beamed back bedroom. A small double bed with a chintzy eiderdown took up most of the room, with a small mahogany wardrobe propped up next to the window and a tiny bedside table the only other furniture.

'If you'd like a bath, it's across the hall. There are fresh towels in the cupboard. I thought we'd go to the pub for supper later. Might be a bit more jolly than staying in.'

In fact Laura had intended cooking at home, but the Moroccan lamb tagine she'd spent most of yesterday preparing was now a charred mess glued to the bottom of a casserole. Even Peggy had turned her nose up at the remnants of her mistress's abortive culinary efforts. The Fox's steak-and-kidney pie beckoned.

'Sounds good,' said Daniel. 'As long as there's wine involved and we can catch up properly. It's really good to see you again, Laura.'

He hugged her. Instinctively she stiffened. Would she ever be able to relax with a man again?

'Good to see you too.'

She left him to unpack. Watching her scurry back downstairs, Daniel wondered if he'd made a mistake coming here.

Perhaps, after so many years, he should have booked a hotel. Or met her in London, as she'd suggested.

Too late now. Hopefully a few drinks at the pub would help her relax.

'So,' Laura giggled, knocking back her third glass of Pinot Grigio. 'Let's talk about your divorce. Tell me all the grizzly details.'

Dinner at The Fox turned out to be an excellent idea. The pub itself was festive and inviting, with a candlelit restaurant, a lively bar and a suitable roaring log fire. Bunches of Kentish hops hung from the low-beamed ceiling, and a delicious medley of smells wafted out from the kitchens, making Daniel's mouth water.

The food so far had been simple but excellent – homemade lentil-and-bacon soup with warm farmhouse bread, followed by a steak-and-kidney pudding of quite ambrosial tenderness. But it was the change in Laura that really made the evening. Whether it was the presence of other people, or the familiar, homely setting, or the copious quantities of wine that had done the trick, Daniel neither knew nor cared. All that mattered was that the awkwardness of this afternoon had vanished, replaced by the sort of easy intimacy only ever enjoyed by very old friends.

'Well,' Daniel began, 'the divorce *is* grizzly. But in a very boring way. You don't want to know.'

'I *do*!' Laura insisted. His face looked even more handsome now there was two of it. 'Did she cheat on you?'

'Actually, I cheated on her.'

'Oh!'

'Yes. Oh. That was what she said, obviously with a couple of other expletives thrown in. Then she took the house, and the children, and anything else she could stuff into her pockets.'

'You did sort of deserve it, though.'

'Yes.' Daniel refilled his glass. 'I was a dick.'

'Who did you sleep with?'

'The au pair. I was a dick and a cliché.'

'Oh!' Laura said again. She couldn't seem to think of any other response. 'Well, er, you're very honest at least. Do you still love her?'

'The au pair?'

'Your wife.'

'Honestly? No. I'm an honest, clichéd dick who doesn't love his wife. Let's talk about you.'

'Let's definitely not,' said Laura, picking up a leftover chip from Daniel's plate and dipping it into the gravy on her own. She was enjoying this evening more than she should be. Good food, good wine and good company had been sorely lacking in her world of late. It was as if God had decided to jolt her out of her miserable stupor by sending Daniel, dropping him back into her life like an unexpected early Christmas present. 'Trust me, you'd be deeply bored. I wouldn't want you to fall asleep at the table before the sticky toffee pudding arrived. The butterscotch sauce here is to die for.'

Right on cue, the puddings arrived, delivered to the table by none other than Lisa James, the Nativity play's Virgin Mary. Judging by the giggling and complete lack of concentration at rehearsals this past week, she and Gabe Baxter were definitely having a fling.

'Here you go.' She set the bowls down on the table, affording Daniel an excellent view of her ample cleavage. Turning to Laura she said, 'Sorry about rehearsals yesterday. I know we was messing about.'

Laura resisted the impulse to correct her – '*were* messing about'. *I must not become my mother.* 'That's all right. It's still early days. Nearer the time, though, you are going to have to take it seriously if you want the play to be a success.'

'I know,' Lisa said sheepishly. Under all the spandex and foundation, she was a sweet girl. 'It's Gabe. He's always been one for the practical jokes. He's a bad influence on me. But I'll get him into line, I promise.'

'Friend of yours?' asked Daniel, watching Lisa James's miniskirted bottom as she walked away from the table.

Laura explained the connection.

'*That's* the most virginal girl in Fittlescombe? I truly must get my act together and move here.'

Laura laughed. 'That's the girl who was stupid enough to accept the starring role in a production full of live cattle and snotty primary-school children. And *this* is the girl who was stupid enough to agree to write and direct it.' She pressed a hand to her chest. 'I must have been out of my mind.'

'I hear you're going to the Furlings Hunt Ball.'

Gabe Baxter had walked up to Laura's table and interrupted her meal without so much as an 'excuse me'. From the look on his face it was clear that his comment about the ball was an accusation rather than an observation.

'That's right,' Laura said defensively, putting down her knife and fork. 'Why, is there a problem with that?'

'A problem? Why would there be a problem?'

'I have no idea. Perhaps you weren't invited and you're irritated that I was. Is that it?'

Gabe laughed loudly. 'Please. I wouldn't go to that love-in for show-offs and posers if you paid me. Who's your boyfriend, by the way?'

He nodded rudely at Daniel, a snide smirk plastered across his handsome face.

'Boyfriend? I should be so lucky,' said Daniel, languidly extending his hand but not getting up. It was a power play, albeit a subtle one, and Laura loved him for it. 'Daniel Smart. I'm an old friend of Laura's. And you are?'

'Gabe Baxter.' It was unspoken, but Gabe seemed suddenly to be on the back foot.

'Gabe plays Joseph,' Laura explained. 'When he's not playing the fool.'

'Lady Muck here doesn't approve of a bit of fun,' said Gabe. 'This is Fittlescombe, not the BBC or the Oxford Bloody Footlights.'

'Actually, the Footlights are a Cambridge society,' said Daniel. Laura could have kissed him. There was just a hint of amusement in his voice, but it was enough to make Gabe's cheeks colour. 'Laura's a brilliant director. A brilliant writer, too. You lot are lucky to have her.'

It was said light-heartedly, and with a broad smile that made it impossible for Gabe to disagree without sounding churlish.

'Yeah, well, maybe. Enjoy your supper.'

I've spent the last two weeks trying to get the better of him, thought Laura. *And Daniel does it in a sentence and a half.*

'He seems a bit chippy,' said Daniel, tucking into his delicious butterscotch-soaked sponge. 'What was that business about the ball? Have you two fallen out?'

Laura rolled her eyes. 'We don't know each other well enough to "fall out". But he's an arse. And *you* just made him look like one. So, thanks.'

'You're welcome.' They clinked wine glasses. Daniel's hand lightly brushed Laura's and she felt her libido switching back on like floodlights in a stadium. She was so buzzed, she was surprised the rest of the pub couldn't hear her humming. 'You're not off the hook, you know,' said Daniel. 'I still want to know what's been happening in your life. Why you left London to hide out here.'

'I'm not hiding,' lied Laura.

Daniel paid the bill. Up at the bar, Gabe Baxter had pulled Lisa James onto his lap and was whispering filthy nothings into her ear. Laura didn't want to watch them, but it was hard not to. Everything Gabe Baxter did was designed for an audience. He simply had to be the centre of attention.

'Let's go home,' said Daniel. 'Leave the Holy Family to it.'

After the noise and bustle of The Fox, Briar Cottage felt eerily quiet. Only Peggy's asthmatic snores broke the silence.

'You must be exhausted,' Laura babbled nervously. 'Would you like a cup of hot chocolate before bed or should I—'

Daniel stopped her with a kiss so forceful she toppled back onto the sofa. The next thing she knew he was on top of her, kissing her passionately and with a fervour she hadn't experienced since . . . well, not for a long time. He smelled of wine and butterscotch and aftershave and sweat. The most delicious smell in the world. Laura felt a jolt of desire so powerful it made her gasp. Then, inexplicably, she blurted out, 'I had a miscarriage. I was pregnant and he dumped me and I got fired and then I lost the baby. That's why I came here.'

Daniel stopped and looked at her for a moment, cupping her face in his hands. 'Poor darling,' he said softly. Without another word he scooped her up into his arms and carried her to her bedroom, laying her down gently on the bed.

'Do you want to be alone? I can sleep in the spare room if—'

'No,' said Laura forcefully. 'I want this. I didn't know if I ever would again, after John. But I do.'

Kissing her cheek, neck and collarbone, moving slowly down her body, Daniel murmured. 'It was the same for me,

25

after Rachel. I was the one who fucked it up, but that doesn't make it any easier. Christ, you're beautiful.'

After that it was all a wonderful, erotic, semi-drunken blur. Daniel peeled off Laura's clothes slowly, but slipped out of his own with the instant ease of a snake shedding its skin. Moments later he was inside her, his body stronger and more powerful than she'd imagined it, his erection gratifyingly large and as solid as oak. Daniel was twenty years younger than John Bingham and it showed. Laura had forgotten sex could be so fast and frenzied, so animalistic and hungry and . . . quick. Just as she was letting go and really getting into her stride, Daniel came, his fingers digging into her buttocks and pulling her hard against him as he yelled out in pleasure.

She hadn't come close to an orgasm herself, but she didn't care. It felt incredible to be desired again, as if she'd been walking around in leg irons and someone – Daniel Smart – had broken the chains.

Wordlessly she curled up in his arms and they both fell into a deep, sated sleep.

CHAPTER THREE

November turned to December, and one of the coldest winters Fittlescombe had seen in a decade. Every morning, village children ran to their bedroom windows, hoping for the much-anticipated snow. Instead they saw a landscape frozen solid, sparkling white with frost like a newly glittered Christmas card. The days were short but dazzlingly bright, a pale winter sun lighting up a cloudless, crisp, sapphire-blue sky. And at night the deep winter blackness was lit by a carpet of stars so perfectly clear it was like sleeping beneath the ceiling of one's own, private planetarium.

For Laura Tiverton, it was the vivid colours of the countryside that most lifted her spirits. The holly leaves and pine trees seemed almost to glow green against the frosted white background of the frozen chalk hills. Berries and robins' breasts seemed redder and the sky bluer than she could ever remember them. In the mornings, Laura would try to write by the fire, but the idyllic view outside her study window never failed to distract her, calling to her like a lover, tempting her from her work. Of course, the fact that she had a *real* lover probably had a lot to do with her revived spirits. Although still not officially an item (he wasn't technically divorced yet), she and Daniel now spoke to each other daily and Daniel had spent all but one weekend since their first night together holed up with Laura at Briar Cottage. They made love, went for long walks and talked a lot about writing – Daniel's writing, mostly. He'd recently finished another quite brilliant play, a comedy, that he was in the process of editing and that would soon be making its West End debut. Laura, meanwhile, had a half-written teleplay full of plot holes gathering dust on her PC. If it was slightly soul-crushing, sleeping with someone so very obviously more talented and successful than she was, the excitement of being in a relationship again more than made up for it. Laura told herself that she would knuckle down to work properly after Christmas, once the Nativity play was over.

With only three weeks to go, play rehearsals were now every afternoon. From one till three, Laura worked with the St Hilda's Primary School children, whose carols and poems would make up the first part of the performance. And, between three and six, the adults came to rehearse, with different actors called on different days to work around people's various job schedules.

Last weekend, Laura had been forced to call a daytime rehearsal on Sunday after church, thanks to so many people missing their weekday slots. Daniel had been a good sport and come along to help, but Gabe Baxter had been so incredibly rude – doing mincing impressions of Daniel whenever his back was turned and flat-out ignoring his stage directions – that Laura had vowed never to bring Daniel again.

'Do you have to be such a prick *all* the time?' she said when she confronted Gabe angrily the next day. Generally, she had adopted a policy of ignoring her tormentor, hoping that eventually Gabe would tire of harassing her and find another sport to amuse himself with. So far, sadly, he showed no signs.

'I don't know what you're talking about,' he said laconically, not looking up from his newspaper.

'Give me that.' To Gabe's amazement, Laura snatched the paper out of his hand. 'You know exactly what I'm talking about. What is your problem with Daniel?'

'I don't have a problem with Daniel. Other than the fact that he's got bugger all to do with this play and should keep his nose out of it.'

'Oh, grow up!' snapped Laura. 'He was trying to help.'

'Well he failed, then, didn't he? It's bad enough having you as a director, never mind your stuck-up, "I'm a big-shot West End playwright" boyfriend showing up to get his ego massaged.'

'You're a fine one to talk about egos,' Laura shot back. 'And what, exactly, is so wrong with having me as your director?'

'Never mind,' grumbled Gabe.

'Actually, I do mind. Your attitude is affecting the rest of the cast; it's affecting everybody. Give me one reason why I shouldn't direct this play, other than the fact that you don't like me.'

'You're an outsider,' said Gabe, snatching back his newspaper. 'All right? You rent a cottage for a few poxy months and you think that makes you Queen of bloody Fittlescombe.'

It was so breathtakingly childish, Laura almost laughed. But one look at Gabe's face made her change her mind.

'I don't think I'm Queen of anything,' she said. 'Harry Hotham asked for a volunteer and I obliged.'

'Oh, I'm sure you're *very* obliging to Mr Hotham,' Gabe taunted.

Ignoring the innuendo, Laura said, 'You should know I don't bully easily, Mr Baxter. I have no intention of stepping aside just to appease your prejudices.'

'D'you use big words like that in bed with Danny Boy? I'll bet that's what gets him off. "Oh baby, say it again! Get out your thesaurus, you know I *love* it."'

'You're pathetic,' Laura said contemptuously.

'And you're blind. He's a fake and a poseur. You don't need an Oxford degree to see that, love. Now are we gonna rehearse or not? Because I've got a farm to run.'

It was a Friday morning, two weeks before Christmas, and the village was alive with excitement. Fittlescombe's festive celebrations had been condensed this year into a single long weekend, with the Furlings Hunt Ball on the Friday night, the Nativity play on the Saturday afternoon of Christmas Eve and Christmas itself falling on a Sunday. Everyone from the postman to the vicar had a part to play, and the sense of goodwill and village camaraderie was contagious.

When Laura stopped into the paper shop for her morning copy of *The Times*, the talk was all of the hunt ball.

'Mrs Worsley was in here the other morning ordering place cards for the dinner. There's going to be over three hundred guests this year. Three hundred!'

'Did you hear that Tatiana Flint-Hamilton's thrown over her duke for a footballer? He plays for Chelsea apparently.'

'Poor Mr Flint-Hamilton.'

'Thank goodness his wife's not alive to see it.'

'You'll never guess who Lucy Norton saw in the chemist's last Thursday. Keira Thingummy-bob.'

'Who?'

'You *know*. The pouty one from *Love Actually*. Banoffee pie? The annoying one.'

'Keira Knightley?'

'That's it. Apparently she's rented Bartley Mill Barn for a *month*! She's coming to the ball for sure, and she's bound to bring all her Hollywood friends. You don't rent a barn that big unless you've got guests.'

Laura half tuned into the gossip as she waited in the queue. What with being so busy with the play, and all the excitement over Daniel, she'd barely thought about the hunt ball. Her invitation included a 'plus one', but the ball was the night before Christmas Eve, and she worried it might look too pushy to ask Daniel to an event on Christmas weekend. He had children, after all, and would doubtless want to spend the holiday with them. Besides, nothing had been said about Christmas plans. He and Laura had only been together (if you could call it that) for a month.

Still, it was a smart event. *I'll need something to wear*, thought Laura. She was going up to London that night to see Daniel. It was his birthday and he'd asked her up to town for dinner and a show, which she took as a positive sign. Perhaps she could squeeze in some shopping while she was there and look for a dress. That way, the subject of the Furlings Hunt Ball would come up naturally.

'That's a pound.'

'I'm sorry?'

'*The Times*.' Mrs Preedy, the shopkeeper, smiled at Laura kindly. 'It's a pound. You're miles away, aren't you?'

'Sorry.' Laura fumbled in her purse for the coin.

'No need to apologize, my love. If I were your age and spending every day rehearsing with Gabe Baxter, I'd spend a lot of time daydreaming too!'

The women behind Laura in the queue all laughed loudly. It was infuriating the way that three-quarters of the village seemed to view Gabe as Fittlescombe's answer to Ryan Reynolds. No wonder the man's ego was so big.

Blushing, Laura paid for her paper. 'Believe me, Mrs Preedy, Gabriel Baxter couldn't be further from my mind.'

'Whatever you say, love.' The shopkeeper winked. 'Whatever you say.'

Rehearsals that afternoon went better than expected. The schoolchildren did a first run-through of their candlelit procession from the school to the church, where the play itself would take place. Laura had confidently expected at least one child's hair to catch fire, *à la* Michael Jackson, but in fact everything went smoothly. Better yet, the reception infants had finally learned the words to all three versus of 'We Three Kings', and had sung something loosely approximating to a tune.

'It's coming together, isn't it?' Laura said excitedly to Harry Hotham, who seemed almost as amazed as she was that his pupils had made such strides. Wearing a beautifully cut wool suit with a yellow silk cravat, his greying hair slicked back, St Hilda's headmaster had clearly made an effort this afternoon. He reminded Laura of a 1950s English film star – David Niven, perhaps. She prayed his smart get-up wasn't for her benefit.

'All thanks to you, my dear.' Harry smiled wolfishly. 'Now listen, what are your plans this weekend? Can I tempt you to dinner in Chichester? There's a new chef at Chez Henri who's supposed to be the best on the South Coast.'

'I'm afraid I have plans.' Laura struggled to hide her relief. 'I'm going up to London tonight to stay with, er, a friend.'

'Ah. The playwright. Smart, isn't it? Lucky fellow,' Harry Hotham said amiably. There was no such thing as a secret in Fittlescombe. 'Still, if you change your mind, you know where to find me.'

At home with your wife? Laura felt like saying. But she held her tongue. After all, she was hardly in a position to judge people for having affairs, not after the wreckage she'd caused by dating John Bingham.

The adults' rehearsal went equally well. Lisa James was sick, no doubt exhausted by Gabe Baxter's insatiable demands, so Laura had to stand in as Mary, reading all Lisa's lines. She'd naturally assumed that Gabe would capitalize on this turn of events and play her up even more than usual. In fact, he was remarkably subdued; a little distant, perhaps, but he made it through the shepherds' scene without a single snide aside or smart-alec remark at Laura's expense. He'd even learned his lines.

'I'm impressed,' Laura told him when they broke for tea and hot mince pies, a Nativity play rehearsal ritual. 'If you're that good on the night, we'll bring the house down.'

'I'm always that good on the night.' He fixed her with the moss-green eyes that had so captivated the rest of Fittlescombe's womenfolk. Laura felt suddenly naked.

'Look, I'm sorry if I've been a bit hard on you.'

'*If?*' Laura spluttered.

Gabe frowned. 'I'm apologizing. Don't interrupt.'

'Sorry. Go on.'

'Actually, that's it. If you want we could have a drink tonight, bury the hatchet and all that.'

Laura looked at him suspiciously. Was this some sort of setup? Some sort of joke? He seemed sincere. The awkward shuffle of the feet, the clumsy way with words. Daniel was a master of communication, firing off witticisms and insights like a champion archer shooting arrows. Gabe Baxter was the opposite, a farmer from the top of his blond head to the soles of his muddy work boots. He certainly wasn't stupid. The annoying truth was that he'd run rings around Laura

33

ever since they'd started this play; he was an expert manipulator. But Gabe was a man's man. Verbal communication was not his strong suit.

Laura decided she might as well meet him halfway. 'That would have been lovely, but I'm afraid I can't tonight. I'm going up to London later for the weekend.'

Gabe's face instantly darkened. 'To see Daniel, I suppose.' He spat out the name like a mouthful of rotten meat.

'Yes, to see Daniel.' Laura stiffened. 'What's wrong with that?'

'Nothing.' Gabe turned away, helping himself to another two mince pies and mumbling 'none o' my business' through a mouthful of crumbs.

Laura was so frustrated she could have hit something, preferably Gabe's broad back, now turned towards her beneath his thick, hole-ridden Aran sweater.

'If you must know, it's Daniel's birthday,' she found herself explaining, unnecessarily. 'We're going to dinner and a show and I'm going to go shopping for a dress for the Furlings Hunt Ball.'

For some reason this got Gabe's attention. 'You're going to the ball?'

'Of course.'

'With him?'

'Probably,' said Laura. 'What do you care, anyway?'

'Oh, I don't care,' Gabe said nastily, his olive branch of a few minutes ago now apparently withdrawn. 'Not in the least. I'm sure you and *Daniel* will have a lovely time shopping in *Harvey Nicks*.' He mocked Laura's accent with ruthless accuracy, laughing as he walked away to join the shepherds on the other side of the room.

Counting to ten to stop herself from screaming, by the time Laura got to eight her mobile rang. Seeing Daniel's name flash up on the screen, she felt her spirits lift. *Fuck Gabe Baxter and his childish mind games. What do I care what he thinks?*

'Hi,' she answered happily. 'I'm just finishing up here. I should definitely make the six thirty train.'

From across the room, Gabe watched out of the corner of his eye as Laura took the phone call. From her smile, and the way she cupped the phone, turning away like a child with a precious new toy they don't want to share, he knew at once who must be calling.

He was angry, at himself more than anything. Ever since they were kids, Laura Tiverton had had the power to unnerve him, to throw him off stride. He'd envied her so much then, with her beautiful house and her happy family and her perfect, Enid Blyton-esque existence. Gabe's parents had divorced acrimoniously when he was eight. The summers that Laura had found so idyllic and perfect, Gabe remembered as times of ingrained domestic misery, of shouting and crying and plate throwing. He was out on his bike all day because he couldn't bear to go home. Against the backdrop of his own, crumbling family, Laura Tiverton's happiness had felt like a personal affront.

And now she was back, beautiful and successful and independent, swooping into Fittlescombe and taking over like a swan returning to lord it over all the ugly ducklings of her childhood. Simply being around her made Gabe feel like a helpless eight-year-old boy again, or at least reminded him of a time that he had spent the last twenty years trying to forget. He knew he was being a dick to Laura, and he didn't like himself for it. But the impulse was too strong to resist. Ever since that prick Daniel Smart had come onto the scene, it had been getting stronger. Gabe distrusted Daniel deeply and instinctively. Everything about him – from his floppy hair, to his smug, entitled manner, to his metrosexual, trendy clothes – reeked of fakery. The fact that Laura couldn't see it, that she so obviously thought the sun shone out of the guy's arse, kept Gabe awake at night. He resented Laura for that, too.

'Shouldn't we be getting back to work?' Arthur McGovern, the sweet old man who ran McGovern's Garage in the village and who had played a shepherd in every Fittlescombe Nativity play since 1988, tapped Laura on the shoulder. 'I'm sorry to nag you, but I promised my wife I'd take her to the pictures in Chichester at six, so I can't be late tonight.'

'Of course, Arthur, my fault. Let's get to it.'

As they walked back to the stage, Gabe noticed the change in Laura's face. Her happiness of a few moments ago had vanished like snow on a warm spring day.

'Is everything all right?' he asked.

'Everything's fine,' Laura snapped. She was growing mightily tired of Gabe's hot-and-cold treatment. 'Let's just get on with it, shall we?'

The rest of the rehearsal seemed to go on for ever, but at last Laura made it to the sanctuary of her car. Turning the key, she blasted up the heat to full and turned on a CD on *Carols from King's*, hoping the soothing choirboys' voices would ease her frazzled nerves.

They didn't. Disappointment and frustration hit her like a double punch to the stomach. Daniel had cancelled. He'd been very sweet about it. Something had come up with one of his sons, the school had asked for a meeting, and he had to go.

'Couldn't we meet afterwards? Or tomorrow, at least?' Laura had asked, hating herself for sounding so needy. But surely a teacher meeting couldn't take up an entire weekend?

'I wish I could, angel, believe me. But Rachel wants us to have lunch on Saturday to talk everything through. Apparently, Milo's grades have fallen through the floor since we split and she's worried about him. I have to show willing, especially with the final divorce hearing right after Christmas. If I don't, she's bound to paint me as a crappy parent in front of the judge. Divorce is so petty and political, you have no idea.'

He was right, of course. Naturally, his son must come first. But Laura still felt robbed. It bothered her how much the prospect of spending this weekend alone, and *not* with Daniel, depressed her. She'd vowed never to depend on a man for happiness again, and yet here she was, depending away, as if all the pain of last year had never happened.

Deciding to take the back way to Briar Cottage, she turned left up Lovett's Lane, which took her directly past Furlings. The house was a Queen Anne gem, one of the finest examples of eighteenth-century architecture in the country. In perfectly square red brick, its façade almost completely covered with wisteria, Furlings managed to combine grand, stately-home proportions with quite unparalleled prettiness. The symmetry of the original sash windows – facing onto formal gardens famous for their topiary, as well as for a two-hundred-year-old maze – was softened by the rolling parkland that surrounded the house on the other three sides. Tonight, lit from within and with its chimneys cheerfully smoking, the house looked as warm and inviting as any fairytale castle. Suddenly Laura realized just how badly she wanted to have Daniel as her date for the Christmas Hunt Ball, to play Prince Charming to her Cinderella. What was the point in spending money she didn't have on a beautiful dress if no one who mattered was going to be there to see it?

Just as she had this thought, there was an ominous splutter from the Fiat's ancient engine and the car quite suddenly lost all power. Thankfully, Lovett's Lane was deserted, and Laura was able to glide to a stately halt on the grass verge. But without headlights, and with nothing but a crescent moon and the distant lights of Furlings to guide her, she could barely see more than ten feet in any direction. Worse still, she'd left her coat back at the church hall, and was woefully underdressed for the December chill in jeans and a thin Uniqlo sweater. Pulling her mobile phone out of her bag, she saw that it was completely dead.

'Fuck!' she shouted out loud, getting out of the car and stamping her foot in anger on the frozen ground like a thwarted child. *Could today possibly get any worse?* The walk home to Briar Cottage from here was about thirty minutes in daylight, but at night and without a torch she was afraid she might not make it all. She could walk up Furlings's drive and knock on the door, but she barely knew the Flint-Hamiltons, and this was an annoyance rather than emergency. The third option was to walk back to the village and ask for help there. Hugging herself for warmth and rubbing her hands together against the cold, she began to trudge down the hill.

After only about a hundred yards, she saw headlights coming her way. *Thank God.* Standing in the middle of the road, she flagged the car down.

'Bit late for a walk isn't it?' Gabe drawled, rolling down the window of his Land Rover. It looked warm and luxurious inside. Coldplay were playing on the stereo, and a smell of new leather wafted out into the crisp night air. 'I thought you were going to London.'

'Change of plans,' said Laura through gritted teeth. Gritted, chattering teeth. 'My car just gave up the ghost.'

'Uh huh,' said Gabe. *Was he smiling? Bastard.* 'I expect you'd like a lift home then, would you?'

Laura nodded grudgingly. *Why, why, why did it have to be* him? *Of all the people who could have driven past.* She tried the passenger door but it was locked.

'Aren't you going to ask me nicely?' said Gabe. He was clearly enjoying himself.

Laura bit her tongue. If she played along she'd be home in the warm in five minutes, as opposed to being stuck out here for the next hour. 'May I have a lift?' She smiled sarcastically.

'Please,' said Gabe. 'Go on. It won't kill you.'

'May I have a lift . . . please?' said Laura.

With a click, the door unlocked. 'Hop in.'

'So,' said Gabe, as she fastened her seatbelt. 'Mr Perfect stood you up, did he? Got a better offer?'

Laura watched his arrogant features break into a grin and felt suffused with loathing. Why was he such an utter, utter dick? And why could nobody else in Fittlescombe see it? OK, so he was handsome in a rough-and-ready, farmhand sort of a way. But it hardly made up for his fatally flawed character, his rudeness, his vindictive streak masked as humour.

'He had a meeting about his son,' she said stiffly. 'It was last-minute and it couldn't be helped.'

'And you buy that, do you?' Gabe asked casually, not taking his eyes off the road.

'I'm not going to dignify that with an answer.' Folding her arms, Laura stared out of the window in silence.

Gabe responded by turning up the music, ejecting Coldplay and tuning into Radio 1. Some awful teen band were playing, one of those Christmas songs with synthesized sleigh bells and cheesy lyrics about snowflakes and children's wishes.

Gabe hummed along tunelessly, strumming the steering wheel in time to the music until at last they arrived at Briar Cottage.

'I'll walk you inside.'

'No, thank you. I'm fine,' said Laura.

'I wasn't asking,' said Gabe. 'It's not gonna be my fault when they find you on your doorstep tomorrow morning, dead from hypothermia because you've forgotten your key.'

The garden path was treacherously icy. In her flimsy loafers, Laura found herself slipping all over the place. Throwing her arms out wildly to try to get her balance, she ended up leaning on Gabe, whose work boots gripped the ice like crampons. Halfway to the door, without asking, he scooped her up under one arm as if she were a stepladder or a Nativity play prop, depositing her on the front step like a Christmas parcel. Blushing furiously, as much from anger as embarrassment, Laura jammed her key in the lock so hard she almost snapped it.

'You might want to invest in some boots,' said Gabe as the door swung open and she practically fell inside. 'And an AA membership. Next time I might not be driving by.'

'Oh no! What on *earth* would I do then?' Laura said waspishly.

Gabe scowled. 'You might be a bit more grateful.'

'And you might be a bit more—'

'What? A bit more what?'

He stepped forward, so he stood just inches away from Laura, his broad shoulders filling the narrow cottage doorway like a marauding Viking warrior. It was a challenge, and Laura's cue to step back, but something kept her rooted to the spot. For a few seconds words failed her. They remained locked in standoff.

'Never mind,' she said eventually. 'To be honest with you, Gabe, I'm cold and I'm tired and I would like to go to bed.'

'Fine. Goodnight.' Gabe turned to go, a look of cold thunder on his face. *Ungrateful cow.*

Just as Laura was about to close the door behind him, resisting with some difficulty the urge to slam it, Gabe suddenly changed his mind. Turning around he said bluntly, 'He's lying, you know. Daniel. He's using you.'

'Oh, my God!' Laura practically screamed with exasperation. 'Using me? Using me for *what*? Daniel's an amazing, talented, phenomenally successful playwright with a flat on Pelham Crescent and God knows how many millions in the bank. I'm an unknown, ex-television writer with a defunct Fiat Punto, a fat dog and an *arsehole* on my doorstep who I'm going to be forced to work with every fucking day between now and Christmas Eve and whose sole purpose in life seems to be to make *my* life hell! What could Daniel Smart possibly, *possibly* want from me?'

For a moment Gabe just stared at her. He'd never seen Laura lose her rag quite so comprehensively before. Her cheeks were flushed apple red, a combination of her high emotion and the biting cold, and her mass of dark curls had escaped their elastic band and fell to her shoulders in a gloriously tangled cascade. The overall effect was disturbingly sexy, but Gabe pushed the thought aside.

'I'm not going to dignify *that* with an answer,' he said coldly. Stalking off down the path, he heard the cottage door slam loudly behind him. *Serve her right if it falls off its hinges in the night and she freezes to death. Stupid, stubborn woman.*

Laura slumped down on the sofa, shaking like a leaf. There were too many emotions to process at once: disappointment, anger, frustration. And something else, underlying all of them, something that she didn't want to admit to. A tiny, poisonous seed of doubt had found its way into her heart, planted by Gabe Baxter and his malicious insinuations.

Had Daniel told her the truth?

She could think of no particular reason why he should lie. And Gabe's motivation was so obviously jealousy – he couldn't stand the fact that Daniel was more successful than he was. Gabe Baxter might be a big fish in Fittlescombe. But in the real world he was a humble farmer, while Daniel was a bona fide theatrical star. Even so, once planted, the doubt was there. Laura resented Gabe for that with a passion that brought her close to tears. Everything seemed to bring her close to tears these days.

Sensing her mistress's unhappiness, Peggy shuffled along the sofa and inserted her wrinkled, piglike face under Laura's arm. Laura stroked her smooth fur gratefully. 'Looks like it'll just be you and me for Christmas, old girl.' Was it weird to put up Christmas decorations that only you and your dog would see? 'Perhaps we'll do Christmas lunch at The Fox,' Laura mused out loud. 'That's a bit less tragic than turkey for one, don't you think?'

The phone made both Laura and Peggy jump. After the miscarriage and her months of deep depression, Laura's London friends had all stopped calling. A ringing phone these days meant her mother, or Harry Hotham calling about the play, or just occasionally—

'It's Daniel.'

Just the sound of his voice was like a shot of pure happiness in the arm.

'Look I'm about to go into this school thing. But I wanted to call and say I really miss you. I'm gutted about this weekend, I really am.'

'Me too,' said Laura, exhaling with relief. The seed that Gabe had planted was already beginning to wither.

'And I was wondering – do say if you think this is too forward, or you're not ready – but I thought maybe the two of us should spend Christmas together.'

CHAPTER FOUR

Daniel Smart walked into Harrods with a spring in his step.

This was going to be a great Christmas.

The last year had been an utter nightmare from beginning to end. The divorce, the bitter end of his affair with Lenka, not to mention the immense stress of producing his most recent play had all weighed heavily. But, quite unexpectedly, fate had brought Laura Tiverton back into his life at exactly the opportune moment. And now here he was, picking up a new dinner jacket to wear to the Furlings Hunt Ball of all things, now only a week away. He felt as excited as a schoolboy about to break up for the holidays. So much rested on this trip to Fittlescombe, but Daniel was ready for the challenge.

Few places on earth were as festive and Christmassy as Fittlescombe village, but Harrods food hall was one of them. As he stepped inside, Daniel's senses were immediately assaulted by the scents, sights and sounds of the season. Wafts of cinnamon and nutmeg drifted over from the bakery, where smiling chefs were cheerfully sloshing brandy into bowls of Christmas pudding mixture. At the confectionary counter, mountains of marzipan glistened in every shape and colour, and sugar mice sported Christmassy red bows, piped in icing around their necks. There were hams and turkeys and huge bowls of glistening cranberry jelly. There were mince pies and candy canes, and vats of piping-hot mulled wine served in bone-china mugs decorated with holly and ivy. Carols rang out through the loudspeakers and everybody, it seemed to Daniel, was smiling.

Picking up a box of German sugarplums for Laura, because the packaging was so exquisite, and a single warm mince pie for himself, Daniel hopped on the escalator up to menswear. Given the pressures on his finances right now, he'd perhaps been hasty in splashing out quite so much for a new, bespoke dinner jacket. But Furlings Hunt Ball was the hottest ticket in England this Christmas, and was bound to be teeming with influential people: writers, producers, actors, investors. Telling himself it was a work expense and tax-deductible, Daniel mentally reduced the price by 40 per cent and pushed the image of his accountant's disapproving face out of his mind.

'I'm here about the jacket. Is it ready?'

The gay assistant looked wounded. 'Of course it's ready, sir. We are never late on our bespoke orders. If you'd like to follow me.'

He led Daniel into a changing room. The jacket, in pure wool and immaculately cut, was duly produced and lovingly slipped onto Daniel's back. While the assistant fussed around him, pulling at the hem and straightening the cuffs, Daniel admired his reflection in the mirror. The deep, true black of the jacket contrasted marvellously with his tanned skin and dark-green eyes, and clever tailoring at the waist accentuated the breadth of his shoulders. It had cost an arm and a leg, but the confidence it gave him was priceless.

'Is sir satisfied? We're quite happy to make further changes if sir feels the sleeves are too long or the stitching at the lapel is a little too fine.'

'It's perfect,' said Daniel.

'It's perfect, Mrs Worsley, absolutely perfect. You've done a marvellous job.'

Tatiana Flint-Hamilton dropped her suitcases in the grand marble hallway at Furlings and beamed at the housekeeper. Tati had known Mrs Worsley since childhood and was well aware of the importance of keeping the old battleaxe sweet. With Mrs Worsley on her side, she had a chance of deflecting at least some of her father's anger. But, with the two of them ranged against her, this unexpected trip home was bound to be a disaster.

'You said you weren't coming.' The housekeeper's face was set like flint. Tati could have struck a match off it to light her much-needed cigarette. 'We rearranged the entire seating plan.'

'I know. The thing is, I was so cross with Daddy about the Bertie thing, I sort of lashed out.'

'*Bertie?*' Mrs Worsley wrinkled her nose in distaste. 'You mean the duke? The married man you took off with, breaking your poor father's heart?'

'Yes, but we're not together any more.' Tati cocked her head to one side and pulled her most adorable *mea culpa* face. It never failed to work with men, but Mrs Worsley was unmoved.

'You upset Mr Flint-Hamilton no end, you know. First the affair, and then writing to him like that, saying you wouldn't bother coming home. You know how much this ball means to him.'

'Which is exactly why I'm here,' said Tati. 'To put things

right.' Her fixed smile was starting to give her jaw-ache. God, Mrs Worsley was a dragon, as humourless as a Glasgow drunk after the whisky's run out. 'Where is Daddy, by the way?'

'Out,' the housekeeper said coldly.

'In that case I'll have a bath and a nap,' said Tati, giving up on the charm offensive. It clearly wasn't working, so what was the point? 'Ask Jenny to bring my bags up and unpack them for me, would you? And please don't wake me. I'll be down when I'm ready.'

Mrs Worsley watched Mr Flint-Hamilton's wayward daughter as she skipped upstairs, as gloriously unaccountable as any spoiled child. With her flowing, honey-blonde hair, high cheekbones and endlessly long legs, Tati had the wild beauty of a racehorse, and the stubborn temperament of a mule. She could be charming when she wanted something, and generous, and on occasion Mrs Worsley had known her to be capable of great kindness. But she was also vain, inse-cure and deeply, deeply selfish, swanning through life with all the entitlement of the very rich and very beautiful. Most of all, she entirely lacked any sense of duty. As duty was her father's lifeblood, this naturally made for strained rela-tions between the two of them.

Rory Flint-Hamilton had hidden his feelings when he received Tati's angry letter informing him that she would boycott this year's ball. But Mrs Worsley could see how saddened and embarrassed he was, mortified by the prospect of having to explain his daughter's absence to so many important guests.

Now, she'd ditched the royal playboy, and apparently divested herself of the unsuitable footballer too. With no new plaything to distract her, she'd decided to show up at the last minute and grace Furlings with her attendance after all.

Tatiana Flint-Hamilton was coming to the Furlings Hunt Ball, and it was obvious to Mrs Worsley what the little minx was hunting for.

'I'm sorry, Tatiana, but it's just not on!'

Rory Flint-Hamilton was as angry as his daughter had ever seen him. Returning from a relaxing afternoon's shooting on the estate (with only twenty-four hours to go before the ball, Furlings was like Piccadilly Circus; he had to get out of the house), he'd come home to discover his daughter sprawled out on the drawing-room sofa eating Maltesers and painting her toenails an unbecoming shade of dark blue.

'You can't just change your mind at the last minute and upset all the arrangements. A lot of people have put a lot of work into this ball.'

'I can see that, Daddy, and the house looks wonderful. I told Mrs Worsley that the moment I arrived. Didn't I, Mrs Worsley?'

The housekeeper's stony silence spoke volumes.

'I haven't come here to cause problems. Quite the opposite. I'll help,' Tati said cheerfully, dripping navy-blue varnish onto the antique Persian rug.

'The seating plan's been finalized.' Picking two sheets of paper up off the Egton sideboard, Rory waved them at her angrily. 'RSVPs were due ten days ago and, if memory serves, you "R'd" in no uncertain terms.'

'I was cross. I didn't mean it.'

'We've got three hundred-odd people coming, Tati. This isn't some family dinner party you can squeeze yourself into at a moment's notice.'

With a sigh, Tati snatched the seating plan out of her father's hand. Scanning it for a moment she said triumphantly 'There. Table twelve. You're a woman short between William Frobisher and the Lord Lieutenant. I'll go there. I'm not fussy.'

'You will *not*.'

William Frobisher was Master of the Furlings Hunt and a devout Anglican, and Jamie Gannon, the Lord Lieutenant of East Sussex, was an arch Conservative and paid-up member of the hang-'em-and-flog-'em brigade. The very idea of Tatiana sitting between these two local luminaries was enough to bring Rory Flint-Hamilton out in hives.

'Fine,' Tati pouted, handing him back the papers. 'If that's the way you feel, if you really can't be bothered to swap one of the women around so your own daughter can come to the dinner, I'll go back to London tonight.'

Her eyes welled with tears. *Bloody little actress*, thought Mrs Worsley. But she could see in Mr Flint-Hamilton's eyes that he was falling for it.

'You can't keep *doing* this, Tatiana,' he said, exasperated. 'Letting people down and then acting as if nothing's happened.'

Unfortunately, despite the strong words, his tone made it perfectly clear that Tatiana *could* keep doing it. That, when it came to her father, all it took was tears and a pleading look and he would eventually crumple like a house of cards.

'I understand. I'll go upstairs and pack.' Tati sniffed.

Getting up from the sofa, spilling Maltesers everywhere, she swept out of the room, bumping into Harry Hotham as he walked in.

'Tatiana, my dear, whatever's the matter?' St Hilda's head-master sensed a Flint-Hamilton family drama with all the relish of a dog sniffing out a juicy bone. Harry had taught Tati as a little girl, but that didn't stop him fancying her madly now. If recent events were anything to go by, she'd clearly developed a penchant for the older man. Perhaps, if Harry could smooth over troubled waters with her father, he'd be rewarded for his troubles. 'You're not crying, are you?'

'Merry Christmas, Mr Hotham.' Tati stifled a sob.

'There, there.' Harry hugged her, shooting Rory a 'what's up?' look over her shoulder. 'I'm sure it can't be that bad.'

'Well, actually, it is. I came home for Christmas, as a surprise for Daddy, but he doesn't want me here!'

'Tatiana, that is *nonsense*,' protested Rory. Mrs Worsley, seeing where this was going and unable to take any more, wisely left the room. 'I merely said that you couldn't expect to come to the hunt ball at a moment's notice. You're perfectly welcome to stay for Christmas.'

'Oh, I'm "perfectly welcome", am I? In my own home! Well, that's good to know,' Tati spat sarcastically. 'I'm welcome to sit locked upstairs in my ivory tower like bloody Rapunzel, while the world and his wife dance the night away downstairs? No, thanks. Can't you talk some sense into him, Mr Hotham?'

'Please, call me Harry. You make me feel so old.'

'All right . . . Harry.' Tatiana giggled coquettishly.

'You are old, you damned fool,' Rory snapped. He considered Harry Hotham a good friend, but watching the old roué flirting with his daughter was enough to turn even Rory's stomach. Happily, Harry didn't seem to take offence.

'I may be old, but I like to think I'm wise as well.' He winked at Tati. 'Life's too short to hold grudges, especially with family. Let Cinderella come to the ball, Rory. I'm sure you can squeeze her in somewhere.'

'I already found a space on table twelve,' said Tati, helpfully.

'There you go, then.' Harry Hotham smiled.

'There you go, my arse. Over my dead body am I sitting Tatiana next to the Master!'

'Well, swap her out for one of the older ladies then, old man,' said Harry. 'Last time I saw the seating plan I'd been put next to Mrs Hotham. Terribly bad form for couples to sit together. Marjorie gets along famously with Will Frobisher. Put those two next to each other, and then Tatiana can sit next to me.'

'Thank you, Harry,' said Tati, kissing her old headmaster on the cheek. 'Come on, Daddy. What do you say? I promise to be on my best behaviour. If I'm not, Mr Hotham will put me straight into detention, won't you?'

Watching his daughter wrap the old fool round her little finger, Rory Flint-Hamilton felt a deep sense of foreboding. Having Tati behave disgracefully in London was bad enough. If she did it in Fittlescombe, Rory's life wouldn't be worth living.

'Fine,' he said grudgingly. 'You can come. But I mean it, Tatiana: I don't want any trouble.'

'I wouldn't dream of it, Daddy,' Tati beamed. 'We're all going to have a lovely Christmas.'

CHAPTER FIVE

Friday, 23 December, was always going to be a big day for Laura Tiverton. It was the day that Daniel Smart was arriving to spend Christmas with her, a huge leap forward in their relationship. It was also the day of the Furlings Hunt Ball. Most importantly of all, it was the dress rehearsal for the Nativity play, an event that had raised Laura's anxiety levels to borderline insanity.

She woke at 4 a.m., haunted by dreams of collapsing sets, children singing out-of-tune carols, live animals running amok through the audience and Gabriel Baxter having disturbingly graphic sex with Lisa James on the straw-strewn stage.

Drenched in sweat, she got herself a glass of water and tried to go back to sleep, but it was useless. The image of Gabe's handsome, mocking face refused to leave her mind. He knew his lines and was perfectly capable of giving a good performance. But he wasn't above messing things up on purpose just to get a laugh out of the audience, or to irritate Laura.

Ever since Laura heard that Graham Kenley, a hugely

successful TV producer with a house in Chichester, would be in the audience (he was in Fittlescombe for the Furlings Hunt Ball, and had a niece at St Hilda's playing one of the angels), she'd been in paroxysms of doubt and terror. Graham Kenley was bound to have heard rumours about Laura's swift, unexpected exit from the BBC. Her name was featured prominently on the programmes as both writer and director of this year's Nativity. That was an embarrassing enough comedown in itself. But, if the play was awful, if Gabe Baxter ruined it, Laura would never be able to show her face in the British television world again.

By six o'clock, exhausted but unable to lie staring at the ceiling a minute longer, Laura had a hot bath, dressed and went down to the kitchen to brew herself a strong coffee. Daniel's arrival had given her all the excuse she needed to go wild with the Christmas decorations at Briar Cottage, which now glittered with more tinsel and baubles than Santa's grotto. Pressing play on her iPod speakers to allow the calming opening bars of 'In Dulce Jubilo' to fill the room, Laura opened the bread bin, tore off a huge chunk of Marks & Spencer's panettone, and lit a White Company 'Winter' candle to lift her spirits. She threw a piece of the sweet bread to Peggy the pug, who ate it, lifting her head momentarily from the comfort of her fireside basket before lowering it again with a disgusted snuffle. It was pitch dark outside and clearly far too early for any sane person, or dog, to be awake.

By the time Laura had cleared away breakfast, plumped the sofa cushions and arranged fresh logs and kindling in the grate (Daniel's imminent arrival had brought on a rare burst of domesticity), the sun had finally peeped its head up over the horizon. Outside, the air was cold and crisp, but the usual blue skies had been replaced by a thick, brooding blanket of clouds. The heavens looked swollen and pregnant with the snow that had been forecast for weeks now. In one way, of course, it would be lovely to have a white Christmas. But fresh-fallen snow would wreak havoc with narrow village lanes. Laura was already having nightmares about half her cast being snowed in, not to mention the audience. After so many months of work, she would not see the funny side if this Nativity play were cancelled.

By the time the dress rehearsal got under way, Laura felt as if she'd been awake for a year. Her nerves, on top of the sleepless night and four enormous mugs of coffee, had left her wired and jittery. Apparently, she wasn't the only one.

'I want a word with you about my boy.'

Gary Trotter, a great, fat slob of a man with a reputation in the village as a bully and a troublemaker, marched up to Laura as the children took their places. Gary's son, the improbably named Denver Trotter, was a chip off the old block, popular at school at least in part because he and his cronies bullied any kids who dared to stand up to them.

'How come Denver ain't got a solo?'

'I'm sorry?' Laura said distractedly.

'You gave the solo to that posh kid. Stick together, your lot, doncha? Well I'm not 'aving it. My lad's got a much better voice.'

'That posh kid' was George Monroe, a shy, nerdy little boy with an absolutely angelic treble. Denver Trotter could hold a tune, but he wasn't in the same league. It hadn't escaped Laura's notice the way that Denver and his mates picked on George. Most of the middle-class families in Fittlescombe sent their children to one of the local private prep schools, but George Monroe's parents hadn't two beans to rub together, so St Hilda's was their only option. With over 80 per cent of the pupils coming from the local village estate, George had struggled to fit in, but his efforts weren't helped by the likes of Denver Trotter.

'Mr Trotter, the auditions were held weeks ago. George Monroe has the solo because he was felt to have the most suitable voice.'

'The poshest voice, you mean.'

Laura bit back her irritation. 'The music department allocated the children their roles, not me. If you have a problem, I suggest you take it up with them, but this is a dress rehearsal. We are certainly not going to reallocate roles now.'

'We'll see about that.' The fat man stalked off.

'What was all that about?' Gabe appeared next to Laura. In his simply fashioned brown woollen robe and sandals, and with a dark beard glued onto his chin, he looked unrecognizable as Joseph.

'Wow.' Laura looked him up and down. 'You look amazing.'

'I look like a knob end. And this bloody beard's itchy as shit,' Gabe grumbled. 'What did Gary Trotter want?'

'Oh, nothing. Just stupid playground politics.'

'The man's a cock,' said Gabe.

'Yes,' Laura agreed. 'He doesn't like George Monroe, or his son doesn't.'

'Why not?'

'Because he's posh.' Laura gave Gabe a meaningful look.

'What are you looking at me like that for? *I* like George. I think he's a sweetheart.'

'Mm-hmm. So people being posh doesn't bother you, then?' Laura asked archly.

'No. It doesn't,' said Gabe, annoyed now that he finally understood her meaning. 'It's people being bossy, stuck-up know-it-alls that I don't like. How *is* Daniel, by the way?'

If the morning had started badly, it was about to get

worse. Someone had overheated the hall, no doubt in antici-
pation of the snow, and the children were wilting under the
bright stage lights. Laura, who'd opted for a new, skintight,
bottle-green, cashmere polo-neck and slouchy wool French
Connection trousers in honour of Daniel's arrival, was
sweating like a Christmas turkey in an abattoir. Her face
had turned an unbecoming shade of red, and her freshly
blow-dried hair already looked greasy and damp with sweat.
The animals fared no better. By lunchtime, one of the heifers,
scared by the spotlights, panicked and lashed out with its
hind legs, destroying the Baby Jesus's crib and putting a
sizeable hole in the wooden stable wall. Lisa James had
fluffed almost all her cues as Mary, and a scuffle had broken
out among the Year Four angels that resulted in George
Monroe falling off the stage and badly scraping his knee.

One of the teachers helped the boy up. 'Are you OK?'

'I'm fine,' said George. Up on stage, Denver Trotter and
his friends had formed a huddle, their whispering inter-
spersed with loud bursts of malicious laughter. Ken Ruddell,
the choirmaster, broke them up, but it was obvious what
was going on.

'Don't let them get to you,' Gabe whispered in George's
ear, taking him aside. 'They're just jealous because you're
the star of the show.'

'Thanks, Mr Baxter. Unfortunately that doesn't help me
much. And the teachers never do *any*thing.' George Monroe
was a gentle soul, but he looked up at his tormentors with
eyes alight with hatred.

They broke at eleven thirty for biscuits and squash for
the children, and a much-needed cup of tea for the adults.
Gary Trotter was still hanging around, ostensibly to help
with the children's drinks and snacks, but actually to
harangue poor Ken Ruddell about Denver having been

robbed of his rightful position of star of the show. Out of the corner of her eye, Laura saw George Monroe reach for a cup of squash, only to have Denver Trotter snatch it up and down its contents in a single, mean-spirited gulp.

'Children can be so cruel,' she observed to Harry Hotham.

'My dear girl, they're animals. Always have been, always will be. There are few environments more ruthless than a primary-school playground, believe me.'

'Spoken by a man who never worked for the BBC,' quipped Laura. She felt awful for poor George, but there was no time to ride to the rescue now.

'Places, everybody! Two minutes to curtain.'

Act Two of the play opened in the now-wrecked stable – *how the hell were they going to get that fixed by tomorrow lunch-time?* – with a set piece involving the shepherds and kings bringing their gifts. Lisa James, centre stage but with nothing to do except nod and smile, began at last to look like a convincing Mary. And Gabe delivered his few lines with no court-jester embellishments. Even the schoolchildren, as the heavenly host of angels, seemed to have pulled themselves together, with Denver Trotter in particular looking subdued.

It wasn't until George Monroe launched into his first verse solo of 'Once in Royal David's City', his pure, reedy treble cutting through the air like the voice of heaven itself, that Laura noticed it. Denver wasn't just subdued. He was grimacing, clutching his stomach. No one on stage seemed concerned. They were all focusing on their own lines and cues. Until suddenly Denver's eyes widened and with a horrified, helpless wail of 'Oh, shit!' he made a run for the stage door. Unfortunately for Denver, a particularly large and obstinate donkey stood between him and salvation.

'Move!' the boy cried. 'Move, for fuck's sake!'

But it was too late. With a fart so spectacularly loud it

sounded like a thunderclap, Denver Trotter's bowels exploded, a thick brown stain spreading across his white angel's robe as splatters of shit sprayed the entire chorus line behind him. Little girls started screaming. The pianist stopped playing, and various teachers ran on stage, flapping their arms uselessly like a flock of surprised chickens. George Monroe, still on his pedestal, kept singing, changing the words to 'Once in Royal Denver's Shitty', and unable to keep the delight off his face.

Laura put her head in her hands. *It's official. The play's a disaster. I'm going to be the laughing stock of Fittlescombe, and Graham Kenley, and Daniel, are going to be there to witness my humiliation first-hand.* Looking up, she saw that Gabe Baxter was clutching his stomach too. Surely the whole cast hadn't got food poisoning? Or some terrible, super-contagious vomiting bug? But then Gabe stood upright and she saw that, far from being unwell, he was actually crying tears of laughter. He winked at George Monroe, and little George winked back.

They did it together! Laura gasped. *They slipped something into Denver Trotter's drink!*

Gary Trotter was on stage now, yelling blue murder. Grabbing his sobbing son by the shoulders he was trying to lead him off stage, when a follow-up thunderclap occurred and Denver exploded for a second time. Unfortunately, this time he was standing right in front of the fan that the stage-hands used to make the angels' wings flutter.

A fine mist of faeces sprayed out across the hall, showering the entire cast with foul-smelling diarrhoea. Even Laura, in her director's chair at the foot of the stage, didn't escape. She was wiping flecks of brown from her ridiculously expensive cashmere sweater when the rear doors to the hall opened and Daniel walked in. In a dashing, floor-length winter coat and Burberry leather driving gloves, carrying a vintage Aspinal of London suitcase and with a beautifully wrapped Christmas present under his arm, he looked like a creature from another planet.

Sexy.

Sophisticated.

Not covered in a ten-year-old boy's poo.

'Jesus Christ.' Pulling out a handkerchief he held it over his nose. 'What in the hell happened?'

Gabe Baxter answered him through tears of mirth. 'The shit hit the fan, Daniel. Bet *that* doesn't happen too often in the West End.'

CHAPTER SIX

Back at Briar Cottage, Laura deposited Daniel on the sofa and raced upstairs to peel off her sweat-soaked, poo-splattered clothes. When she saw her face in the bathroom mirror, she had to stifle a sob. She looked a fright. Her cheeks were beet-red, her nose had gone all shiny, and strands of limp, greasy hair stuck to her forehead like tendrils of seaweed clinging to a rock. Heavy bags under her eyes attested to last night's lack of sleep and a hellish day of rehearsals. The Furlings Hunt Ball would get under way in a matter of hours, attended by a raft of stunning, perfectly groomed women. Apparently, Tatiana Flint-Hamilton had come home for the event, on the lookout for a new lover and determined to outshine all the competition.

She won't have to try very hard to outshine me, Laura thought miserably. *I'm going to look like such a frump*.

What on earth had possessed her to bring Daniel to the ball as her date? If he hadn't already realized how far out of Laura's league he was, tonight was sure to bring the point home to him.

Oh well. Too late now.

Jumping into the shower, slathering cinnamon body scrub onto every inch of her skin, and washing her hair twice with extra-shine shampoo, Laura tried to push today's disastrous dress rehearsal out of her mind. It was well known in theatre lore that the best productions had the worst dress rehearsals. Perhaps today was actually a good omen. Everything that *could* go wrong *had* gone wrong. Tomorrow's performance could only be better.

It was only Daniel's presence that had stopped Laura having a knockdown, drag-out fight with Gabe Baxter, who clearly thought the whole Denver Trotter incident hilarious.

'You put something in that boy's drink, didn't you?' Laura had hissed at him, pulling him aside backstage.

'I don't know what you're talking about.'

'Pull the other one. I know Denver isn't the most likable child . . .'

'He's a bloody menace.'

'But he *is* a child. What you did was completely uncalled for.'

To Laura's amazement, Gabe actually had the temerity to lose his temper with *her*. 'Oh? And who made you the judge of what's called for and what isn't? That lad's been bullying poor George for weeks now, and no one's done a damn thing to stop him. Those teachers at St Hilda's should be shot.'

This was one point on which Laura agreed with him. The teachers should have stepped in, but none of them dared face the wrath of Denver's father.

'Whatever you may think about me, Miss High and bloody Mighty, I am not a snob. I was sticking up for the Monroe boy, posh or not.' And with that Gabe had turned on his heel and stomped off, without even offering to help clean up the mess he'd made.

Forget him, Laura told herself, climbing out of the shower and drying herself, rubbing hard at her scalp to try to wake herself up a bit. *Forget the lot of them. Tonight's about me and Daniel, nothing else.*

Half an hour later, she came downstairs to find Daniel kneeling on the window seat, with his head outside.

'Listen.' He beckoned her over. 'How lovely is that?'

The church bells of St Hilda's were pealing, a rich, layered sound ringing out through the cold night air. It was pitch black outside, so there was nothing to distract the senses from the ancient melody other than a lingering smell of wood smoke.

'They're practising for the Christmas Eve carol service,' said Laura. Washed and scented, with her freshly dried hair hanging loose and glossy down her back, she felt a lot better than she had earlier; although she still wished that her burgundy velvet dress didn't feel quite so tight. If she ate too much at dinner tonight, her bodice was in serious danger of popping open and giving the gentlemen of the Furlings Fox Hunt more than they'd bargained for.

Closing the window, Daniel slipped an arm around her waist. 'You look amazing.' He kissed her, pressing his lips to hers, then moving slowly down her neck and collarbone to the tops of her spectacular breasts. Laura shuddered with desire.

'We could always skip the ball,' she whispered, running a hand through his thick, chestnut hair.

Daniel laughed. 'And waste that beautiful dress? I don't think so.'

Laura hid her disappointment as he stood up and stretched, scratching Peggy's ears before retrieving his suitcase.

'I'll go up and change,' he said briskly. 'Won't be long. Then we can have a couple of gin and tonics before we set off.'

Furlings's Great Hall shimmered in the candlelight like a brightly jewelled palace. Everyone agreed that Mrs Worsley and the Ball Committee had outdone themselves this year, and that the house had never looked more spectacular. Constrained as ever by Rory Flint-Hamilton's tight hold on the purse springs, the hunt wives had sensibly gone for a Victorian Christmas theme. Expensive ice sculptures had been replaced by simple but striking arrangements of holly berries and dark-green foliage. Walls were hung with ivy and mistletoe and clove-stuck oranges, instead of pricey artificial decorations, and gaudy electric light fixtures had been eschewed in favour of more than a thousand simple church candles, twinkling like living stars on the walls, windowsills and every available surface.

The tables, dressed with plain white linen, made the perfect backdrop for the spectacular Flint-Hamilton silver, polished to burnished perfection by the kitchen staff till it gleamed and danced in the candlelight. Red glass bowls of dates and brightly coloured sugared almonds added a dash of colour, and throughout the house a rich, pungent smell of mulled wine filled the air. Flames leaped up in the huge, baronial fireplace, where a pile of pine logs as tall as a ten-year-old child crackled cheerfully. And, in all four corners of the room, Christmas trees cut from the estate woodlands, and decorated only with candles in clear glass baubles, stood like sentries, welcoming guests to the feast.

Most of the locals came early, eager to start the merry-making and to catch the first glimpse of this year's celebrity guests. The Home Secretary and his wife were coming, as were Hugh Grant and his new girlfriend, and the Hollywood actress Mia Celeste. Keira Knightley pleased everyone by arriving early with her fiancé, James Righton *and* both of the Miller sisters. And the new English cricket captain showed up, fresh from his Test victory in the West Indies, looking tanned and gorgeous and, rumour had it, newly single.

'Laura, my dear. You look a vision.'

Harry Hotham sidled up to Laura and Daniel, reeking of aftershave and looking as happy as a puppy in a steakhouse as a string of stunning young women wandered past. Beside him, his long-suffering wife Marjorie wore the expression of a woman who would have much preferred to be at home watching *Gardeners' World* or listening to a Mahler symphony on Radio 3. In a sensible, knee-length floral dress and flat shoes, with her hair pulled back in an eighties-style bow and wearing no make-up at all other than a slick of bright-pink lipstick, she reminded Laura of her own mother.

I must call her, she thought guiltily. She'd been so consumed with the play, and Daniel, and her writing, she'd barely spoken to her parents in months.

'You'd better keep a tight hold of her, Daniel.' Harry winked amiably. 'Or one of these young bloods will whisk her away.'

Daniel laughed thinly. He wasn't really listening. Looking over Harry's shoulder, he seemed almost awestruck by the glamorous guests who kept arriving, slightly to Laura's surprise. She'd assumed he attended smart events like this all the time.

'I mean it,' Harry said to Laura. 'You're the belle of the ball.'

'Thank you, Harry,' Laura said politely, despite the fact that this was a blatant lie. The famous actresses looked ravishing, of course, but so did any number of the local girls, almost all of whom were slimmer and sexier than Laura. Even Lisa James, who was here not as a guest but to serve cocktails, was attracting a huge amount of male attention in her short black dress with the feather-fringed skirt. Watching her, Laura was astonished to see Gabe Baxter, squeezed uncomfortably into a dinner jacket and trousers, heading over to the bar and whispering something lewd in Lisa's ear.

How did he *get invited? After all the stick he gave me about the Furlings Ball! What was the expression he used? 'A love-in for show-offs and posers.'*

Turning around to ask Daniel if he'd excuse her for a moment, she found he'd already wandered off somewhere. Grabbing a fresh glass of champagne from a passing waiter for Dutch courage, she made her way over to where Gabe was standing.

'Fancy seeing you here,' she said archly.

Gabe looked her up and down, his eyes visibly lingering on her bust, straining for escape from its maroon velvet prison.

'I got a last-minute invitation,' he told Laura's breasts. 'One of the whippers-in is a mate of mine.'

'Really? And here was I thinking that you wouldn't be seen dead at this "love-in for posers". I can't imagine where I ever got *that* idea from.'

'It's like an illness with you, isn't it?' Gabe said hotly. 'You have to be right about everything.'

'At least I'm not a raging hypocrite, claiming to hate the upper classes then wangling your way in at the last minute to guzzle the lord of the manor's champagne!'

Gabe flushed deep red. 'You stupid cow. I came because . . .' He left the sentence hanging.

'What? You came because what?' Laura challenged him. 'I'd like to know.'

'Never mind.'

For a few moments they stood there in awkward, charged silence. Then Gabe said, 'Your boyfriend seems to be enjoying himself.'

Laura turned around, following Gabe's gaze. Daniel was on the other side of the room, next to one of the Christmas trees, chatting animatedly to a beautiful blonde in a backless silver dress. The girl seemed glued to what he was saying, leaning forward and touching his forearm every few moments in a distinctly intimate gesture. Now it was Laura's turn to blush.

'He isn't my boyfriend. We're only dating casually,' she heard herself saying.

'So I see,' said Gabe. 'Well, you enjoy your night.'

He walked off, leaving Laura alone by the bar, watching Daniel. It was true they had not officially made a commitment to each other. She'd told herself she was happy to wait – Daniel was still mid-divorce, after all – but she realized now with a sharp pang that this was untrue. That she'd allowed things to continue on a vague, casual basis out of fear. After what had happened with John, she couldn't bear the thought of being rejected again.

This realization was painful enough. But having to hear the truth from Gabe Baxter was an even more bitter pill.

Feeling Laura's eyes on him from across the room, Daniel looked up and smiled at her. Making his excuses to the blonde, he came over.

'Who was that?' asked Laura.

'Katie Crippin. She's a wonderful stage actress. I met her last year, after—'

'You were flirting.'

Daniel frowned. 'Don't be silly.'

'I'm not being silly. You were flirting with her, right in front of me.'

'Are you jealous?' Daniel smiled. When Laura didn't smile back he grew serious again. 'Where did all this come from?'

'It came from you flirting.' Laura jutted her chin out with a braveness she didn't feel. 'I don't like it. I . . . I want us to be exclusive.'

Just at that moment, the Reverend Slaughter hobbled over and started talking to Laura about tomorrow's Nativity play, launching into conversation loudly and insistently, the way that only the very elderly and very deaf are able to do. There was nothing for Laura to do but nod and smile and watch helplessly as Daniel was sucked back into the throng.

'We'll talk later,' he mouthed, over the Reverend's bald head.

Oh God, thought Laura. *Oh God, oh God, oh God. I've blown it.*

'. . . don't you agree, Miss Tiverton?' With a start, she realized that Reverend Slaughter was still talking.

'Oh, yes, definitely.'

'So you'll make the changes?'

'Erm . . .'

A loud gong reverberated through the Great Hall. *Saved by the bell.*

'Dinner is served!'

Dinner was delicious – smoked-salmon rillettes with horse-radish sauce, succulent roast beef with all the trimmings, and a Christmas pudding so drenched in brandy it should have come with a health warning – but Laura barely took a bite. Instead, in despair at having so rashly overplayed her hand with Daniel, and feeling fat and uncomfortable in her tight burgundy dress, she drowned her sorrows in Rory Flint-Hamilton's excellent vintage claret. Daniel was seated at a table so far across the room she'd have to crane her neck just to catch a glimpse of his back. Meanwhile, some sadist had sat her between Gretchen Lewis, St Hilda's school librarian and officially the most boring woman in the village, and Lord Lomond, a Scottish grandee in his eighties with a gammy leg and foul temper to match. Ignored by both of them, Laura allowed the good wine to work its magic, becoming contentedly glazed as she watched the glamorous guests, admiring the huntsmen's red frock coats and mentally rating the women's dresses on a scale of one to ten. She was just thinking that Hugh Grant's girlfriend looked the prettiest of all of them – in a short red halter-neck dress and spectacular matching boots, like a porn Little Red Riding Hood . . . *Little Red Riding Hooker*, Laura thought and laughed, spilling claret down the bodice of her dress – when the most stunning girl she had ever seen in her life swept into the room.

In a floor-length, nude silk dress, slashed to the thigh and completely backless, and with her perfectly streaked honey-blonde hair piled on top of her head like a crown, Tatiana Flint-Hamilton glided across the room like a goddess. Through her semi-drunken haze, Laura wondered where she'd been until now. Hiding upstairs in her bedroom, just waiting for the right moment to make an entrance? If so, that would make her a raging narcissist. Then again, how could you not be if you looked in the mirror every morning and saw *that* staring back at you? Her photographs didn't come close to doing her justice.

To Laura's horror, she saw that Tatiana was seated at the next table to Daniel. As she approached, he stood up and pulled out her chair for her. Laura watched, frozen, as the two of them kissed on the cheek and exchanged a few words, Tatiana laughing at some comment of Daniel's before she sat down and was immediately pounced upon by Harry Hotham.

They know each other.

It was clear from both of their body language that Daniel and Tatiana Flint-Hamilton had met before.

Why didn't he say anything to me?

Dinner was almost over and the live band were taking their places, ready for the start of the dancing. There were to be reels and some old English country dances – Strip the Willow, the Dashing White Sergeant and the like – followed later by a traditional disco. Carriages were officially at midnight, but in previous years the Furlings Ball had been known to go on until dawn, with the younger generation drinking and partying long after the oldies had gone home to bed. With the play tomorrow, Laura would have to make an early night of it. She longed to get away, to somehow take back what she'd said to Daniel earlier, go back to Briar Cottage and make love until everything was all right again. But, if she tried to drag him home too early, she risked looking even more pathetic and desperate. *I must stay, and dance, and act as if nothing's happened. Nothing* has *happened. I should never have let Gabe Baxter get to me. So what if Daniel was flirting with that actress? And so what if he's met Tatiana Flint-Hamilton before? None of that means anything. He came here to spend Christmas with* me. *I have to get a grip.*

Standing up to go to the loo, Laura had to clutch the back of Lord Lomond's chair to steady herself. The whole room swayed gently, like a boat at anchor. Perhaps she should have eaten some of her pudding. So much wine on an empty stomach had clearly gone to her head.

Focusing intently, both on where she was walking and

on not glancing towards Daniel, she made her way out of the Great Hall and into the corridor. It was cooler out here, and quiet, and the change of atmosphere soothed her. With no signs indicating where a loo might be, Laura headed upstairs. A sash window on the landing had been partially opened to let in some crisp night air. Through it, Laura could see thick, heavy snowflakes falling and felt a childish delight. However inconvenient it might be to her adult self, with the play scheduled for tomorrow, there was a magic about snow, and particularly Christmas snow, that could not be denied. It meant purity and hopefulness and the promise of a bright, white future, a fresh start. It was what she had come here for, she and Peggy, back to Fittlescombe, to the place she'd been happiest. Not Daniel Smart, nor Gabe Baxter, nor John Bastard Bingham could take that away from her.

Upstairs, with nothing looking obviously like a bathroom, Laura started opening doors. Most of the rooms were bedrooms and had clearly not been redecorated for decades. Chintzy Laura Ashley wallpaper suggested a woman's touch at some point back in the 1980s. Laura found herself wondering when, exactly, Tatiana's mother had died. She must have been very beautiful to produce a daughter like that.

The style of the rooms was old-fashioned and simple, with nothing to suggest the family's vast wealth. Most of the furniture was solid Victorian mahogany, and the odd water-colour painting hanging on the walls was the only attempt at adornment. Rugs were Persian and tatty, and the beds were made up with sheets and blankets rather than duvets, giving them a look of a boarding school dormitory.

Bedroom, bedroom, bedroom. Laura was starting to wonder whether there were any bathrooms at all, or if

Furlings's guests simply peed out of their windows, when the fourth door opened and a distinctly dishevelled Lisa James fell out into the corridor, giggling.

'Oh! Hello.' She blushed when she saw Laura. 'I was just . . . we were, erm . . .'

Gabe Baxter sauntered out behind her. His shirt was untucked and he was wiping away very obvious lipstick marks with a handkerchief.

'Hi,' he said to Laura, unsmiling.

'I was just looking for the loo,' she found herself explaining. For some reason she was blushing furiously, as if it were she who'd been caught *in flagrante*.

'Well, you found it,' said Gabe tersely. Taking Lisa's hand he led her towards the stairs.

Shutting the bathroom door behind her and locking it securely, Laura undid the hook and eye on her dress and sank down gratefully onto the loo. It felt wonderful to be able to breathe and enjoy the cool sensation of porcelain against her skin. Less wonderful were the livid red welts around her ribs from where her bodice had dug into her skin, not to mention the familiar feeling of tension that seemed to follow every encounter she had with Gabe Baxter. Laura didn't know what it was about Gabe. How he always managed to throw her off stride. All she knew was that she felt foolish around him, as though she had a giant piece of spinach permanently stuck to her teeth. And her stomach was full of something. Not butterflies – that was far too pretty an image. Something *like* butterflies, but unpleasant. Moths. Or bats.

With an effort she pulled herself together, refixing her hair in the mirror and wiping away an unfortunate mascara smear with a piece of tissue. For one awful moment she feared she was going to be physically unable to winch herself back into her dress. But, after much frantic tugging of fabric and sucking in of the stomach, she succeeded in refastening the hook and eye and yanking up the zip. Feeling a bit more sober, tossing back her mane of dark curls with a confidence she didn't feel but was determined to project, she walked back along the corridor towards the stairs. But after a couple of paces she froze.

She heard them before she saw them. Daniel's voice, low and enticing, the voice that only a few hours ago had been whispering in her ear at Briar Cottage, telling her how gorgeous she looked. And a female voice, higher but completely confident, the cut-glass accent ricocheting off the stairwell walls like shards from a broken chandelier.

'Are you sure no one's up here?' Daniel asked.

'If they are, they shouldn't be. Why? Are you ashamed to be seen with me, darling?'

'Ashamed? Are you kidding? Every man in that room wanted you. I'm the lucky bastard who won the prize.'

It was too late to run to back into the bathroom. Panicked, Laura flattened herself against the wall, like a toddler playing hide and seek who believes that, if they close their eyes, no one will see them.

Miraculously, Daniel didn't see her. He was so mesmerized by Tatiana Flint-Hamilton's cleavage, and so focused on bundling her into the bedroom, he probably wouldn't have noticed if a *T. rex* were running down the hall. Looking over his shoulder, however, Tati saw Laura, back to the wall like a sentry on duty, and winked. It wasn't a mean wink. Quite the opposite. It was matey and conspiratorial, a 'we're all girls in it together' wink. *She has no idea who I am*, thought Laura. *Daniel never told her he came with me.* She stood, rooted to the spot as Daniel rattled the doorknob behind Tati's bare back and finally got it to open. With loud shrieks of delight, the pair of them shot into the bedroom and out of view.

Laura didn't know how long she stood in that corridor. She didn't remember how she got downstairs, who she passed on the way, or how she retrieved her coat from the cloakroom. But at some point she found herself standing outside in the snow, about halfway down Furlings's drive, staring at the village lights below her like a sleepwalker emerging from a terrible dream.

It must have been snowing for at least three hours, as the ground was already blanketed with white. Behind her, sounds of music and voices and revelry hung faintly in the air, like a distant echo. But around her, and in front of her, all was peace and white and silence. The world had been muffled, softened, muted. Laura wished she could do the same to the voices inside her head. *You're a fool*, they mocked her. *A complete fool.*

'Hey.'

Gabe Baxter's feet crunched heavily through the snow. He had no coat on, but had run down the drive in just his dinner jacket. White flakes stuck to his hair and glittered on the lapels of his jacket like sequins. He looked handsome and freezing and as totally out of place as a snowman in a sauna.

'Are you OK?'

'Please go away.'

'I saw what happened. Everyone saw the two of them sneak off together.'

'For fuck's sake!' Laura spun around, her sadness and embarrassment and disappointment suddenly condensed into anger. Anger at Daniel for being a snake, anger at herself for being a fool, but most of all anger at Gabe Baxter for just *being*. 'What is your problem? You followed me out here, like some kind of weird stalker, just so you can gloat?'

Gabe shivered, wrapping his arms around his chest against the cold. 'Is that what you think? That I came out here to gloat?'

'Well, didn't you?'

'Unbelievable.' Gabe shook his head, kicking at the snow with irritation. 'I tried to warn you, you know. I knew he was a user.'

'You knew nothing!' Laura shouted. 'You were jealous, that's all. So don't bother trying to dress it up as concern for my welfare.'

'Jealous?' Gabe's eyes widened with outrage. 'Of that tosspot? I don't think so.'

They stood in awkward silence for a moment. The snow began to fall faster and thicker, till Gabe's shoes were completely submerged in white.

'Look, it's fucking freezing,' he said, breaking the silence because one of them had to. 'I'll drive you home.'

'No!' Laura sounded angrier than she meant to. But she couldn't be around anyone at the moment, certainly not a man, and *certainly* not Gabe Baxter. There was only so much humiliation a girl could bear in one night. 'Go back to Lisa. I'm sure she's back in the warm right now, waiting eagerly for round two.'

'You know what? Fine,' said Gabe, matching Laura's anger with her own. 'Maybe I *will* go back to Lisa.'

'Good.'

'Great. At least we agree on something.' Gabe began walking back towards the house. But after a few paces he stopped.

'You know,' he said to Laura, 'for someone who went to Oxford, you can be painfully fucking stupid sometimes.'

'Tell me something I don't know,' said Laura, turning her face away so that he wouldn't see her tears. Gabe might have seen Daniel Smart make a fool of her – the entire village might have seen it – but that was one satisfaction Laura wasn't about to give him.

Holding her head high, she walked on through the snow towards the village without looking back.

CHAPTER SEVEN

Laura walked into St Hilda's church hall with a fixed smile plastered on her face.

'My dear. Merry Christmas Eve!' Harry Hotham greeted her warmly, making no reference to the large pair of sunglasses she was wearing to cover eyes puffy from crying, nor to the supersized flask of coffee she clutched to her chest like a security blanket. 'There's no need to worry about anything. The entire cast are present and correct, a minor miracle if I do say so myself. Now that you're here, the only thing we still need is an audience.'

'Merry Christmas, Harry. Everyone.'

It wasn't a Merry Christmas, of course. It was the worst, most shaming, crushing, awful Christmas Laura could possibly have imagined. By now the entire village, school and probably half the county knew what had happened last night. That Laura's date for the Furlings Hunt Ball, her big-shot London playwright boyfriend, had publicly dumped her in favour of the stunning Tatiana Flint-Hamilton. The two of them were probably still shacked up at Furlings right now. Either that or they'd already jetted off to some exotic location to begin their glamorous lives together. Meanwhile, Laura was here, in a church hall full of excited schoolchildren, nursing the sort of hangover that merited a call to the paramedics at the very least, if not immediate admission to rehab.

She'd considered not showing up tonight. Burrowing deep under her duvet and staying there until the snow melted, or her heart mended, or at least until she could stand up without wanting to throw up. But, after a morning spent staring at the ceiling and weakly sipping Alka-Seltzer, she realized that the show must go on. Not just tonight's show. But *the* show, the tragicomedy that was Laura Tiverton's life. *That* had to go on, whether she wanted it to or not.

'What happened to the set?' she asked, as the musicians began a warm-up rendition of 'Good King Wenceslas'. Someone had brought mince pies and a huge vat of mulled wine backstage for the adult performers, and the smell of sugar and alcohol wafting over made Laura feel violently ill. 'That crib was in pieces last night.'

'Gabe Baxter came in at crack of dawn this morning and repaired everything.' Harry Hotham smiled. 'We've rechristened him the Angel Gabriel.'

I wouldn't go that far, thought Laura, watching Gabe flirting with the make-up girl as she daubed foundation on his cheeks at the side of the stage. But it was a very kind and thoughtful gesture, especially given what time he must have got to bed last night. She remembered their conversation in the snow last night word for word, and wondered now whether maybe she'd been too hard on him. It was at least possible that he'd followed her down Furlings's drive out of concern.

Downing the dregs of her coffee, she walked over to him.

'You fixed the set.'

'Yup. You showed up.'

'Yup.'

They looked at one another awkwardly. It felt as if there should be more to say, but Laura at least couldn't think of what it might be. In the end Lisa James broke the tension. Resplendent as Mary in a full-length blue robe with a white nun's wimple and headdress and a frighteningly convincing baby-bump sewn into her midsection, she came over to ask Laura about her lines in the kings-and-shepherds scene. Laura noticed the way Lisa turned her back to Gabe, making a point of ignoring him.

'Have you two had a row?' she asked Gabe afterwards.

'Not really. We broke up last night.'

'Oh! I'm sorry.'

'Don't be. It wasn't going anywhere. She knows it really, she's just annoyed I beat her to the punch. Listen, do you have a minute?'

Laura glanced around at the throngs of children and teachers and set hands all needing direction. 'Not really.'

'Yes, you do. It won't take long.' Grabbing her hand, Gabe led her through one of the rear stage doors into a corridor at the back of the building. A couple of shepherds were going over their lines at the far end, but otherwise the two of them were alone. 'I want to talk about Daniel.'

Laura stiffened. 'That makes one of us. Truly, Gabe, I don't have time for this right now. People will start arriving soon, curtain goes up within the hour and—'

'He's bankrupt.'

Laura paused for a moment. 'He . . . what?'

'This is all about money. He's bankrupt, in debt up to his eyeballs on his latest play. He's been trying to screw cash out of every rich heiress he can get his hands on in London

78

for almost a year now, but it wasn't enough. That's why he came to Fittlescombe.'

Laura tried to take this in, not easy through her thick hangover fog. 'But that makes no sense,' she said eventually. 'He came here to see me. *I'm* not a rich heiress. I can barely afford to pay my water bill.'

'Yes, but Tati Flint-Hamilton is. Remember when he first contacted you? It was the day after you were invited to the Furlings Hunt Ball, wasn't it?'

'Yeeeees,' Laura said cautiously. 'But I don't see what—'

'You posted about it on Facebook,' said Gabe, 'didn't you? And the very next day, good old Daniel Smart decides to look you up. After ten years. It wasn't you he came here for, Laura. It was never you. It was always Tati. He wanted a chance to get close to her and you gave it to him.'

Laura's eyes narrowed. For a moment all her old distrust of Gabe came rushing back. 'How do you know all this? What do you know about Daniel's finances and his motives?'

'I know a lot. I didn't trust him from the day I met him and I decided to check him out. Just because I'm a farmer doesn't mean I'm a moron, you know. You don't have to go to bloody Oxford to recognize a liar when you see one. It only took a couple of calls to discover his play was up shit creek. He hadn't told you that, which got me thinking, "What else hasn't he told her?" Turns out it was a fuck of a lot. He'd been after Tati for months, but she kept sodding off abroad with her rich lovers, giving him the slip. Last night he finally pinned her down.'

Literally, thought Laura.

Was it really true? Had Daniel really been using her from day one? She scanned Gabe's face, searching for traces of insincerity, but found nothing.

79

'Why?' she asked him at last. 'Why did you bother finding all this out? I mean, why did you even care?'

The question obviously angered him. 'Because, you stupid bloody woman,' he shouted, 'I—'

'Sorry to interrupt, guys.' Eileen Carter, one of the St Hilda's teachers, ran in, flapping her hands like a distressed bird. 'But I need Laura. The first load of parents just arrived, Michael O'Brien's got stage fright and is refusing to put on his wings, and I'm afraid to say our cellist, Mrs Kennedy, has had one too many glasses of mulled wine and has just been *extremely* rude to the bishop.'

'You'd better go.' Gabe's face shut down like a mask. Laura didn't know why, but she felt a surge of disappointment mingling with the nausea and nerves.

'Yes.'

She followed Mrs Carter back into the hall. Everything else would have to wait for now. It was show time.

By the time the curtain went up and the Fittlescombe orchestra (minus one cellist) launched into the first, rousing strains of 'Deck the Halls', St Hilda's church hall was packed to the rafters. Parents, parishioners and villagers of all ages sat eagerly in the front rows, many of their faces known to Laura since childhood. Suddenly, last night and Daniel and all the bad things that had happened melted away. It had been a terrible year. But Laura was happy to be here, in this village, in this hall, surrounded by these kind, familiar faces. She belonged in Fittlescombe in a way that she had never belonged anywhere else. She was proud that it was *her* play, *her* work that the village had turned out to see on this cold, snowy Christmas Eve.

After yesterday's disastrous dress rehearsal, Laura held her breath throughout most of the first act, but it went off without a hitch. The carols sounded magical, with George Monroe's solo performance raising the hairs on everyone's forearms with its purity and beauty. Even the reception infants did a terrific job, getting through 'Away in a Manger' without forgetting the words or having their wings fall off or needing to be taken to the loo. Act Two was where most of the drama came in. Laura had put her own stamp on the classic Nativity story by trying to give Mary and Joseph a more real, believable marriage. There was lots of dialogue between the two of them, and some banter that had worked well in rehearsals. But she was scared that, after last night's break-up, the onstage spark between Gabe and Lisa might fall flat.

Again, for once, the gods were with her. With the lights and attention on her, and the whole village watching, Lisa James suddenly emerged from her cocoon like a gloriously unexpected butterfly. Before, it was Gabe who had got all the laughs. But tonight Lisa displayed a comic timing and pathos that Laura had never imagined her capable of.

'She's a real actress,' she whispered admiringly to Harry Hotham backstage. 'Who'd have thought it?'

'She has wonderful material to work with, my dear. Not to mention a great director.'

Laura kissed Harry on the cheek. He was an incorrigible flirt, but his heart was in the right place. She realized she had grown quite fond of him.

Almost before she was aware of it, the final scene came to an end and the curtain came down to riotous, wild applause from the audience. As the orchestra struck up 'We Wish You a Merry Christmas', the cast walked back on stage for their bows. First came the children, angelic and rosy-cheeked, flushed with their own success. Then the shepherds and kings. The innkeeper and King Herod, played by the local greengrocer and butcher respectively, got a huge cheer. And finally Gabe Baxter and Lisa James, hand in hand and smiling broadly, walked out for their encore.

In the wings, Laura was clapping and whooping as loudly as anyone when Lisa James suddenly marched over and dragged her out onto the stage.

'Oh, no, really,' Laura protested, aware of what a fright she must look. 'No one wants to see me out there.'

'Course they do. We all do,' said Lisa.

And it was too late. With the spotlights blinding her, Laura stood awkwardly between Lisa and Gabe as the crowd roared their approval. Grabbing her hand, Gabe raised her arm, then pulled her down into a deep bow. As she bent over, the hairband holding back her tangled curls fell out, and Laura's hair cascaded everywhere. To her utter horror, she realized too late that it wasn't a hairband at all but a pair of knickers. She'd been in such a state this morning, she must have grabbed the closest thing to hand. She lunged forward to retrieve them but Gabe was too quick for her, snatching up the offending garment in a millisecond and stuffing it into his pocket. Then the curtain fell for a final time and the stage lights went down.

Hugging Laura warmly, Lisa James skipped off to join the rest of the cast in the dressing rooms, leaving Gabe and Laura alone.

'Yours, I believe.'

He pulled the scrunched-up knickers out of his pocket with a grin.

Blushing furiously, Laura grabbed them from him. 'It's not funny.'

'Of course it's funny! It's bloody hilarious.'

'Do you think everybody saw?'

'No! Not from that distance. It could have been anything, a scarf or a hankie or whatever. Anyway, who cares?'

I care, thought Laura. But she didn't have the energy to fight about it.

'We're all going to The Fox to celebrate. Are you coming?'

Laura shook her head. 'I'm wiped out. I'm going home to bed.'

'Oh, come on, you can't,' said Gabe. 'It's Christmas Eve. You should be out having fun with all of us, not brooding at home on your own about arse-face.'

'I won't be brooding,' Laura lied. 'And I won't be on my own. I've got Peggy.'

Gabe looked as if he were about to say something, then thought better of it.

'Fine,' he shrugged. 'Suit yourself. You know where we are if you change your mind.'

Outside in the car park, Laura scraped the snow off her windscreen and was about to start the engine when a man tapped her on the shoulder.

'Oh my goodness!' she jumped. 'You scared me.'

'Sorry.' The man smiled. He was tall and distinguished-looking, despite an ill-judged, holiday-themed sweater with a holly motif and a tiepin that flashed 'Merry Christmas' every few seconds. 'I just wanted to say that was a terrific performance. I've been coming to the Nativities at Fittlescombe for the last fifteen years, but what you put together was in a league of its own.'

'Oh. Thank you,' said Laura, adding nervously, 'It's a good job you didn't see it yesterday. It was a bloody disaster then, believe me. We all got covered in diarrhoea. Ha ha ha!'

For a moment the man looked startled, unsure what to

say to this last unexpected revelation. Then he pulled out a business card and pressed it into Laura's hand.

'Yes, well, call me. I understand you've been working on a new script for television. I'd like to read it. And, er . . . Merry Christmas.'

The man walked off, rejoining a group of friends. Only when Laura got into her car, turned on the heating and the inside light, was she able to read the name on the card.

Graham Kenley
Gable Productions

With all the drama about Daniel and Tatiana Flint-Hamilton, and the stress of tonight's production, she'd totally forgotten that Graham Kenley was going to be in the audience.

He liked my play!

He wants to read my script!

My script? What am I talking about? I haven't got a script. She'd been so consumed with Daniel Smart and fantasies about their future together, Laura had barely typed a word in months.

Driving home far faster than she should have on the slippery, snowy back lanes, Laura burst into Briar Cottage, lit the fire, fed Peggy and sat straight down at her computer. All her earlier tiredness had gone. For the first time in months she felt alive creatively, energy and adrenaline coursing through her veins like an electrical current through a wire. She started to type, words flowing out of her like water from a spring. Once she started she couldn't stop.

She was so engrossed that at first she didn't hear the knocking. It was only Peggy's barking that woke her from her reverie. Irritated, she got up and opened the door.

'Hi.'

Daniel stood on the doorstep. He held a bunch of hand-tied red roses in one hand and a light-blue Tiffany box in the other. A light dusting of snow made his hair glisten. His teeth were perfectly white, and his handsome face flawless beneath the glow of the porch lamp.

'Look, I know I've been an arse. A total arse. And I know I hurt you. But it's you I want, not Tatiana. Can I come in?'

Five minutes later, sitting beside the fire listening to Daniel, Laura felt as if she were in a dream.

'I'll admit it,' Daniel said. 'I was blinded by her celebrity. And obviously, you know, she's pretty.'

'Obviously,' said Laura.

'But, as soon as I woke up this morning, I knew I'd made a terrible mistake.'

'Why was that? Because she didn't give you the money you needed to bail out your play?'

Even Daniel had the decency to look shamefaced.

'Money *was* part of it. I've been under so much financial pressure, Laura, you don't understand. But that wasn't the only thing. I didn't intend to fall in love with you. But I have, and last night made me realize that.'

'Mmm hmm.'

Laura looked at Peggy, who made her feelings clear by farting loudly. *I agree*, thought Laura. Daniel went on.

'Tati flew to Kitzbühel a few hours ago. She's got some rich bloke out there, evidently. But I don't care. All I want is to be with you, here. To have Christmas together like we planned.'

'But Daniel,' Laura said slowly. 'You dumped me in front of three hundred people. You slept with someone else.'

'To be fair,' said Daniel, taking Laura's hand in his. 'We

hadn't made a commitment to each other. You said as much yourself last night. We weren't exclusive. But I'd like to be now. If you knew how much you mean to me Laura . . .'

With a jerk, Laura withdrew her hand, as if she'd been stung by a bee.

'I know it'll take time.'

'Daniel?' Laura said softly.

'Yes?' Daniel's handsome face lit up with hope and expectation.

'Get out of my house. Get out before I throw you out and never, *ever*, come back.'

The loving look in his eyes soured like curdled milk. He stood up, slipping the Tiffany box back into his pocket and throwing the flowers down churlishly on the table.

'Fine. If that's how you feel.'

'That's how I feel.'

'You're making a big mistake you know, Laura,' he said nastily. 'It's not as if you have so many other, better offers on the table.'

Laura sighed heavily. What had she ever, ever seen in him?

'Fuck off, Daniel!'

With a slam of the door he did.

For a moment Laura stood rooted to the spot, listening to the roar of Daniel's engine as he drove away. Then she laughed out loud. What a dickhead! What a total and utter dickhead. She contemplated going back to her writing, but the moment had been lost. On a whim, she put on her coat and boots and walked out into the snow.

She wasn't sure where she was going. Not to The Fox. She wasn't in the mood for socializing. She just felt a need to be outside and walking and *free*. Above her the dark night sky twinkled with stars, and the smoke smell from her own fire hung deliciously in the crisp air. The lane shone bright white with compacted snow, and all around the hedgerows and scenery were laden with thick frosting, a true winter wonderland. It wasn't actually snowing at this moment and there was no wind, which made for a pleasant walk. After about a quarter of a mile, she was close enough to hear noise from the village and was on the point of turning back when a familiar voice startled her.

'Laura? What are you doing out so late? Are you all right?'

Gabe Baxter loomed in front of her like a big, broad statue emerging suddenly from the darkness.

'I'm fine. I just felt like a walk. I thought you were at the pub.'

'I was for a bit.' He came closer, so Laura could make out his features in the moonlight. The broad jaw, broken nose and mischievous eyes were the same as they'd always been, but something in Gabe's expression was different. 'But then I remembered I needed to do something.'

'What did you need to do?' asked Laura.

'This.'

Grabbing her around the waist with both arms, he pulled her to him and kissed her, hard and strong and for a very, very long time. He smelled of whisky and stage make-up and his stubble felt rough and scratchy against Laura's cheeks. This was nothing like kissing Daniel. Or John. Or anyone she'd ever kissed before. This was pure magic.

'Come with me,' he said, when at last they came up for air, grabbing her hand and leading her over to a stile at the side of the road. With his hands on her waist again, he lifted her over into the snowy field as if she weighed no more than a straw doll. Hidden from the road, but only a few feet back was a barn. Unbolting the door, Gabe pulled Laura inside.

'Aren't we trespassing?' she giggled.

'Nope. This is my land.'

Gabe pulled a torch out of his coat pocket and wedged it between two hay bales to give them a little light. Then, taking Laura's face in his hands, he kissed her again, more gently this time. Removing his coat, he placed it over the straw. Then he rolled up his scarf as a pillow and, scooping Laura up into his arms like a groom carrying his bride over the threshold, laid her down gently on the makeshift bed.

Gazing up at him, stroking his face with her hands, Laura wondered how long she'd wanted him and realized that it had been a very, very long time.

'So.' She couldn't seem to stop smiling.

'So.' Gabe smiled back, and slowly began to undress her.

In the distance, the bells of St Hilda's began to ring out, summoning the villagers to midnight mass. The sound mingled with Gabe's breathing as he pulled off his shirt and expertly unfastened Laura's bra. She had never felt happier in her life.

It was going to be a very Merry Christmas indeed.

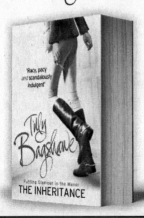

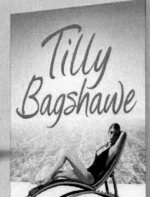

Master storyteller Sidney
through

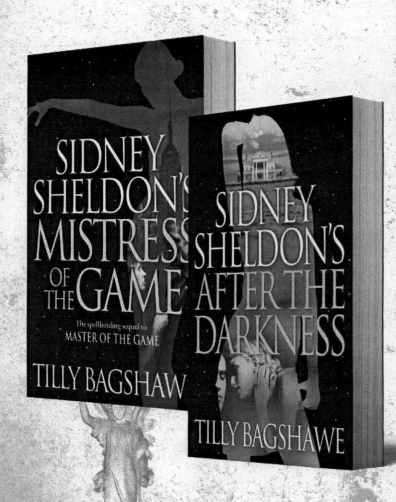

Sheldon's legacy continues
Tilly Bagshawe

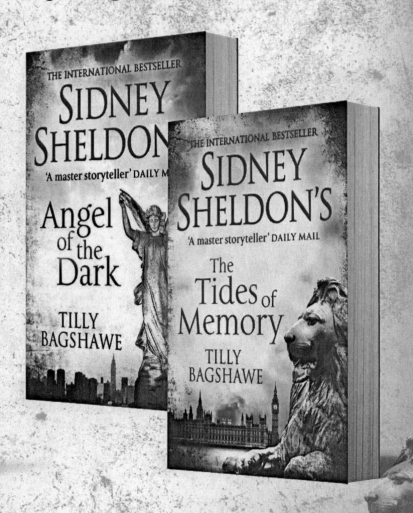

Keep up to date with

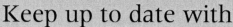

www.tillybagshawe.com

Find Tilly on Facebook

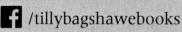 /tillybagshawebooks